Children of Albion Rovers

To Martin and Judith

On your wedding day

Davy Bell and Derin

"Children of Mid-Argyll"

Donna and Susan

All the Best!

Children of
Albion Rovers

Edited by
KEVIN WILLIAMSON

First published in Great Britain in 1996 by Rebel Inc., an imprint
of Canongate Books Ltd, 14 High Street, Edinburgh EH1 1TE

Extract from 'Wonderwall' by Oasis, reproduced by
kind permission of Creation Records

Editor: Kevin Williamson

British Library Cataloguing in Publication Data
A catalogue record for this volume is available
on request from the British Library

ISBN 0 86241 626 4

Typeset by Palimpsest Book Production Limited,
Polmont, Stirlingshire
Printed and bound in Finland by WSOY

Contents

TEAM TALK 1

Pop Life BY GORDON LEGGE 5

After the Vision BY ALAN WARNER 29

The Brown Pint of Courage BY JAMES MEEK 67

Submission BY PAUL REEKIE 95

The Dilating Pupil BY LAURA J. HIRD 135

The Rosewell Incident BY IRVINE WELSH 171

Children of Albion Rovers

TEAM TALK

PICKING A TEAM is never easy. Different managers have different criteria. The late great Jock Stein would put it all down to pub arithmetic. And for him everything turned out sweet as a nut. Genius is not about doing the simple things well but the complex things simply. When John Lambie took over the managerial reins at Falkirk you could see the truth stripped bare. He learnt the hard way. Previously, he'd invested heavily – although not financially – in workaday journeymen during his spell at Partick Thistle. Honest jobbers with steel toe-caps. Yet at Brockville the formula cracked. Stars in their eyes. Copycat criminals. There was much guilt at the wake. Napoleon, geeing up his troops on the eve of battle, once remarked: *morale is to the physical as four is to one*. He was right. But that was his Waterloo. John Lambie could've learnt a bit more between hairdos.

I have my own methods, a minister once said to me. I think he was a Methodist. Well I too have my own methods. It's no use just signing star strikers. That's a recipe for disaster. I've learnt from the Souness years that you have to build from the back. Chris Woods and Terry Butcher. That's when the tide turned. I've never admired Graeme Souness more than when he left the celebrations of a Rangers victory over arch-rivals Celtic – on April 1st 1990 – to go to an Anti-Poll Tax concert at Edinburgh's Usher Hall. He watched the proceedings with his wife from a seat in the balcony. See? Build from the back. Every time.

To this end I've selected an international keeper and a class A defender – both of whom I have total faith in. Irvine Welsh – a keeper of the faith. And Alan Warner – a defender of the faith. They are the smooth and charismatic spinal column of the team. They've learnt how to cope with the pressure – and the vagaries of the press – producing performances the fans just rave about. The world is at their feet and they know how to pass.

There is much running about to be done in midfield and a wide expanse of the pitch has to be covered. A cool eye for situations is prerequisite. This position needs more than just realism. Midfield needs imagination and pop mobility. The ability to fly at will. Selflessly. Players who sparkle. Like Johnny Doyle. You know the sort. What's that? Gordon Legge and James Meek you say? Sorted. Proven track records at every level. They come recommended and are adaptable to both Premier Division and Tennent's Sixes.

Up front, if we're going to have any impact on the new league set-up, we're going to need fresh legs. Strikers whose tricks and feints haven't been studied in depth by the efficient but essentially Night Nurse opposition. The Andy Ritchies and George Bests rather than the Linekeresque bores. Forwards who don't pollute the beautiful game with their predictable technique. Aye. Fuck the dullards with a Gerry McNee boner. Laura Hird and the boy Reekie are on from the start.

So that's it. The Children of Albion Rovers FC. Bodies honed to the very peak of fitness by years of substantial training. Shirts on their backs. Trophy room bare. But this team is Going Places! Ooh aah.

Kevinacchio Vilhelmsonya
(Continental-Style Coach)

Pop Life

GORDON LEGGE

IT ALL STEMMED from their problems. With Martin it was money, with Ray it was women and with Hilly it was . . . well, it was always a wee bit more complicated with Hilly.

See Hilly was the sort of bloke that would take offence; and that was about the size of it. All that was needed was for somebody to say something, something commonplace, something you'd hear any day of the week, and next thing Hilly would be heading for the door, slating the others for being nothing so much as 'spoilt bastards'.

That was what had gone wrong the last time, the last time the three of them had got together.

They'd been round at Ray's one night when Martin, as he always did, started going on about his latest financial crisis. In the course of this, Martin had happened to come away with the one about how the more you earn, the more you spend. Hilly made a joke of it at first. The joke being that if Martin had a million pounds in his pocket, then chances were the million pounds would disappear before Martin reached the end of whichever street it was Martin happened to be walking on – with nothing to show for it, no recollection of what he'd done with it. But then Ray went and made the mistake of agreeing with Martin, saying that once you reached a certain level of income you never seemed to be noticeably that much better off. That was enough for Hilly. He did his 'spoilt bastards' routine and stormed off.

It was a good six months before Hilly had anything more to do with either of the other two. Six months in which Hilly was seen to hang around with the Kelsey's or the Kerr's, usually pissed or stoned, always laughing his head off.

Hilly was like that. When he was in a bad mood, he went out, he became more visible.

Ray, on the other hand, was the exact opposite, when Ray was in a bad mood, he kept himself to himself.

For years Ray had put up with the others going on about their successes and their conquests as far as women were concerned. Every so often all this would get to Ray; and, every so often, it would be Ray's turn to slip out of the scheme of things.

Because he never really knew what he wanted from them, Ray was hopeless with women. Honestly, it was like watching a body trying to eat who didn't realize the food was supposed to enter via the mouth. Hilly and Martin told him as much. There was even a time when they figured it was as well to tell the truth as anything: and told Ray that no woman they knew actually liked him. But before they'd had the chance to develop that, to talk it through to an extent that may actually have been of some kind of benefit, Ray made his excuses and left. He never blew up or anything, that wasn't his style, he just, as Hilly put it, turned out the lights. Subsequently, the only times you'd ever catch sight of Ray were out late at night, out jogging, weights strapped to his wrists and ankles.

Back when they were younger, Martin had been the first to leave school. At a time when everybody they knew was signing on, Martin was changing jobs at the rate of one a month: dishwasher, labourer, that kind of thing. Even so,

Martin was always short of money, always asking for loans. To his credit, he did pay back; but he was never the one to turn up at your doorstep and say, 'Here's that money I owe you.' No, Martin had to be hunted down, and you had to embarrass yourself by asking for what you were rightfully owed. Likewise, it wasn't unusual to be out with Martin, and for some complete stranger to come over and demand money from him. Such instances rattled Ray and Hilly. Consequently, Martin would get slagged to bits, be made to feel really rotten, to such an extent that it would prompt Martin's hiatus. Martin, though, didn't storm off like Hilly, or turn in on himself like Ray. No, what Martin did was to run away. Martin fucked off. He would somehow manage to borrow twenty quid off somebody or other, then disappear off to the city, or away down south, or, on two notable occasions, over to the continent.

But it wasn't just the borrowing Martin did: Martin sold things. One time that was really annoying was when Martin sold his Bowie collection. He hadn't even sold it to a collector, just some dud at a record fair for about a tenth of what it was worth. All he'd got in return had amounted to little more than a good night out. But that wasn't the point, the money wasn't the point, the point was *you didn't sell your records.*

For it was records that had brought them together in the first place. At school, they'd noticed the same names scrawled on each other's bags, books and desks. From there they'd got to talking. Soon, they were exchanging records and making up tapes for each other. It wasn't long before the three new friends were spending all their free time sat in front of each other's speakers, appraising their own collections, investigating their brothers' and sisters'; talking about nothing other than records.

Whilst everybody else of their generation seemed content to spend Saturday mornings hanging round up the town, giving it the best bored teenager routine, Martin, Ray and Hilly treated Saturday mornings as though they were on a no-frills, top-secret assignment. They'd head up the town, straight to the record shop, browse for exactly twenty minutes, make their purchases, then head straight back home.

It was a truly amazing time; discovering all this great music, getting overwhelmed by it. And the great thing was it wasn't a case of one liking this, the other liking that – what one thought the others were thinking, what one said the others agreed with. In as much as they ever could be the same, they were the same: they dressed the same; they did the same things; they were all in the same boat as regards money, women and opinions.

Then, just as they were getting their interviews with the careers advisory woman, punk rock happened.

Initially, it was great. More great records. Records, in fact, that were even better than a lot of the stuff they'd been listening to. It was a discovery again. Only this time round, it was a discovery they could call their own. This time, they weren't out hunting for records; this time, they were waiting for records.

Yet while Martin, Ray and Hilly were equally keen to embrace the new, they responded to it in completely different ways. For Martin it meant party, it meant always going out, having to try everything: every drug; every fashion; every possibility. Performance was what attracted Ray, being on stage – the forlorn hope being that women were only just waiting to fling themselves at the feet of the local axe-hero. For Hilly it became as important to state what he didn't like as much as to state what he did like. So while Martin would be all excited, looking for a party, looking for the action, going, 'What's happening? What's happening?' Ray would be thinking about his band, and, being a bit unsure, would waffle on something about, 'Don't know. Supposed to maybe be a gig in a couple of months. All depends, though . . .' Hilly, on the other hand, God bless him, was never too bothered with having to think about things. Hilly just started every second sentence with the then trademark words, the italicized '*I hate* . . .'

And there you had it, the three friends: the hedonist, the hopeful and the hostile. Whenever Ray landed a gig the situation would transpire that Martin wouldn't turn up because he hadn't the money, while Hilly wouldn't turn up cause he thought the band were crap.

Responses that not surprisingly got right royally on Ray's nerves.

Not that Ray was ever the one to talk, mind, not when it came to getting on folks' nerves, anyway.

Thing was, Ray would always be leeching around in the hope of meeting up with women. He spent a small fortune treating Martin, going to this pub, that club, chasing parties here, heading round there. Not that it ever achieved the desired purpose. Martin was so restless, such a party animal, that by the time they got served somewhere, or got accepted somewhere, Martin would be on about where they would be going next, where they could be going that was better. Come the early hours of the morning, when everyone else was heading home, Martin and Ray would still be stopping off at the cash machines, stocking up for that elusive good time.

Ray was also into pestering Hilly to go out. A mission which was as doomed as any mission ever could be. See Hilly was never much of a mixer. Hilly's idea of a good night out was to sit in the same seats of the same pub with the same faces he always sat with, talking about the same things he always talked about. When Hilly was in company he didn't care for, he said so; when Hilly was in a place he didn't care for, he left.

Over the years things went on like this. The three friends got on with their lives but, increasingly, struggled to get on with each other. Martin married a rich man's daughter, Hilly married a lassie who lived three doors away, Ray never married. Ray could, however, lay claim to being the most well off, seeing as how he became an administrator for the region's education services. Martin worked for the health board in a self-advocacy project while Hilly earned his crust with a family-run removal firm.

Despite the changes that entered their lives, and the fact that, by this time, they were hardly ever seeing anything of one another, Martin, Ray and Hilly continued to share a bond that came from them spending so much time together when they were growing up. When two of them bumped into each other, they invariably spent most of their time talking about the third – often to the exclusion of even talking about themselves.

On those rare occasions when the three *did* get together, it was only a matter of time before they broached the subjects they never liked to talk about, only a matter of time before one of them upped and opted for the early bath.

Even though the others were never in the slightest bit interested, Martin would always contrive to go on about his money problems. He didn't get much sympathy. The fact that Martin never had anything to show for all this money that mysteriously disappeared was too much for Hilly. The fact that Martin admitted to nicking money from his wife, and denying money to his wife, was enough to send Ray off.

Ray was by far and away the wealthiest of the three. Ray knew this, and didn't like it one little bit. The others never intended it as such, but whenever Martin went on about the ease with which Ray accumulated his wealth, or when Hilly went on about what he saw as the pointless possessions Ray had a habit of acquiring for himself, Ray felt they might as well have been having a go at his failure with women – he was rich because he was alone.

But while Martin and Ray at least admitted to having problems, Hilly never would. There was nothing wrong with Hilly. If folk couldn't handle a few home truths then that was their problem. These self-styled 'home-truths' covered everything from the mildly embarrassing right through to the downright ignorant. The mildly embarrassing was when Hilly was in the home of somebody he considered middle class. In such circumstances, Hilly would always make a point of pilfering something, usually from the drinks cabinet, occasionally from the bathroom, but always something expensive, always something that would be missed. The downright ignorant side of Hilly showed with his penchant for having a go at Martin and Ray, and folk close to Martin and Ray. Hilly was a bit of a wind-up merchant, where nothing was ever practical, everything was a matter of principle. As long as Hilly was having a good time he wasn't the one to care. Martin and Ray couldn't stand it. It would always end up that one of the three would up and leave.

Then, following the 'the more you earn, the more you spend' incident, two whole years passed without the three of them being together. They only ever saw each other in the passing, down the town or going to the games. As for getting together, arranging something; well, they didn't really see the point. It was as though they'd gone through a bitter divorce; they associated each other with their problems and that was that. The memories just seemed to be bad memories.

As time wore on, though, it was the normally self-assured

Hilly who came to realise just how much he missed the other two. Hilly had no fervour for socialising or meeting new folk. Hilly had such a dislike of most folk, anyway, that it was pointless him even contemplating going out and finding new mates. Sure, he got on with the folk at his work and with his family but somehow, something, was missing.

And Hilly knew what it was. His two friends. Martin and Ray. Hilly wanted to see them again. Properly. He wanted the three of them all to get on with each other.

Hilly thought about it, about how they were all doing away fine on their own but how they couldn't get on when they were together. It was then Hilly had an idea, the same idea he always had. When things weren't working out, then you went back to the way things were when they did work out.

Hilly contacted Martin and Ray. He told them how they should all meet round at Ray's on the first Tuesday of the following month. The idea being that they would only talk about records. Seeing as how that was what had brought them together in their youth, there was no reason why it shouldn't continue to be the case. They would bring along their new purchases, play them and talk about them. On no account were they to talk about anything other than records.

In love with the romance of the idea as much as anything, Martin and Ray said yeah, they were willing to give it a go.

And that's what they did.

Unfortunately, though, the first occasion proved to be little short of a disaster. True to form, Martin hadn't brought anything. He said he hadn't had the money. Ray, meanwhile, had brought damn near everything. He'd even brought along stuff he hadn't yet played. Hilly was furious with him. After about two-and-a-half seconds of each record, Hilly would go on about how crap it was, slagging it to bits, and slagging Ray for having more money than sense. Hilly himself was the star of the show, playing his records and enthusing about them.

The next time round was better. Throughout the month Martin had stayed in, listened to all the decent radio programmes, latched onto something that was brilliant and bought it. Ray and Hilly agreed, it was a classic. Ray himself had spent his lunchtimes hanging round the record shops, listening to what the kids were wanting to hear, and buying the best. It was mostly dance but it had a power and urgency that won over the others. Hilly, as was his want, took his cue from what the papers were raving about. Yet even he had to concede that what Martin and Ray were playing was as good in its own way as the stuff he normally listened to.

And that set the precedent. Martin listening to the radio, Ray hanging round the record shops and Hilly reading his papers. They held their monthly meetings, and they never talked about anything other than records.

At first they'd been concerned that what they were bringing along was good enough, making sure there wasn't some little reference that would draw the derision of the others. But, in time, they grew confident. They had a pride in what they were buying. Equally, they were keen to hear what the others were buying.

Before long, they began to notice changes in each other. Martin had started off by coming along with just a couple of singles, but now he was appearing with a few singles *and* a couple of LP's. Not only that but people in the streets had been stopping Ray and Hilly to ask for Martin. Nobody was seeing much of Martin these days. They'd all assumed he'd gone a-wandering again. But no, Martin was around. Martin was doing fine. Simple truth was Martin wasn't going out because Martin didn't want to go out. He wanted to stay in and play records. Many's the time he'd got himself ready to go out but he always had to hear just one more record, then another, then another. It ended up with Martin having to ask himself the question: what did he want to do, did he want to go out, or did he want to stay in and play records? So Martin stopped going out.

The change in Ray had to do with his appearance. Whereas Hilly had always dressed classically (501's, white t-shirts) and Martin went in for the latest Next or Top Man high street fashions, Ray always looked as though he was going to a game in the middle of January. Now, following their Tuesday nights, Ray was taking a few chances, and it was paying off. He was looking alright. He was getting his hair cut every six weeks instead of every six months. His flat seemed different as well. It was more untidy, yet it was less filthy. It looked like he was living there rather than just staying there.

The big change, though, was with Hilly. Martin and Ray were always wary of Hilly, knowing that Hilly was perfectly capable of dismissing their purchases – and, by implication, themselves – with either a subtle shake of the head, or, by going to the other extreme, and bawling and screaming his socks off. But Martin and Ray were so into what they'd bought, so passionate about it, that they did something nobody else could ever be bothered to do: they argued with Hilly. Nobody ever argued with Hilly. Folk usually just ignored him, or laughed at him, nobody ever argued with him. But Martin and Ray did – and they won. They won him over. They got him to listen to what they were playing, *and* to listen to what they were saying.

On a couple of occasions they almost broke the rules. There was one time when Hilly was so excited he'd phoned Ray up at his work, telling him how he had to go out and buy something.

Ray had said no, it had to keep, there were rules to be obeyed. Another time they'd all turned up with virtually the exact same records. Martin seemed uncomfortable. But he didn't say anything. Next time round, Martin appeared with the same number of purchases as he'd had the previous month. He said that yes, the notion had entered his head just to turn up with a batch of blank tapes, but that he'd decided the important thing was to own the records. That was what it was like when they were younger, that was the way he wanted it now.

The three friends still argued, of course; but they only ever argued about records. They argued about what made a good record, whether something ephemeral could ever possibly be as good as something that was seminal. They argued about whether bad bands could make good records. They argued the case for Suspicious Minds being better than Heartbreak Hotel. They argued with passion, with loads of logic, even with blind prejudice – but they never held back, never kept their thoughts to themselves.

Hilly had long held the belief that the place for dance music was the dancefloor. Not that he was bigoted against it or anything, just that playing records that went beep-beep thwack-thwack in the privacy of your own home was about as pointless as playing 95% of live LP's. But he came to understand, through force of sheer enjoyment as much as anything, that the records could stand on their own, that they were as valid and wonderful in their own way as the stuff he normally listened to.

As for Martin; well, it wasn't so long since Martin had all but stopped buying records. Occasionally, he'd've got something from the bargain bins, but he wasn't involved, he was purchasing out of a sense of obligation rather than want or need. Now he was buying things full price. Not only that but because he was taking his cue from the radio, he was ordering the likes of expensive imports and limited edition mail order. Martin's disposable income was still short in terms of its lifetime, but now at least there was something worthwhile to show for it.

Likewise with Ray. Prior to the arrangement, Ray had been the one blanding out. When it came to music, what he'd been buying had been predictable – comfy compilations, bland best sellers. He'd even bought a CD player. But, after a few meetings, he'd gone back to vinyl. Like he said, he'd got the taste again, and owning vinyl was like tasting chocolate.

It was as if they'd gone back to the old days, back to their youth. But they knew the only way to get the most out of records was to hunt them down, to be obsessive. See that was the great thing about records: you never just went out and bought the best, you had to discover the best. As much as the powers that be had tried to market so-called 'classics', records weren't mere things you owned, like accessories, and said, 'I've got it,' like you'd say you'd 'seen' a film or 'read' a book.

As agreed, the three friends continued to have nothing to do with each other other than the monthly nights round at Ray's, and then they only ever talked about records – they never talked about themselves, they never gossiped, they never discussed what was happening in the news. Originally, this had meant that they wouldn't be bringing up their problems, letting their personal lives interfere with their friendship. The strange thing now was that they were all doing fine. But they didn't tell. Martin had bought a house, Ray was engaged to be married and Hilly had become a father. Most folk thought it was Hilly's parenthood that had turned him into a more reasonable bloke, but Martin and Ray liked to believe it was the time they spent together, listening to their records and talking about them, that had brought on the change that meant, for the first time, Hilly actually appeared to be interested in folk when he was talking to them.

Over the festive season there was no exchange of presents or even cards, instead the three friends compiled lists of their records of the year, compared them, and analysed those that were in the papers and those featured on the radio. During the summer they timed their holidays so's not to coincide with the first Tuesday of every month. There was no illness or problem that kept them from their appointments. They were never late, nobody ever left early.

The summer was always a lean time for new releases. In view of this, it was agreed to forego the norm and have an evening in which they brought along lists of their all-time favourites. Top two hundred singles, top hundred LP's. For the whole month they never went out. Wanting to be as sure of their lists as they could, they stayed in and played and played and played.

It proved to be a great night. Easily the best yet. So many records they'd forgotten about. They'd had near-enough identical top fives but after that it was just classic after classic after classic. The lists were beyond dispute. It was almost scary that there were so many great records that they all knew off by heart, that they all knew so much about. Thinking about it, there had to be thousands. Those they'd listed had only been a fraction. The lists had been too limiting. Next time round – if there was to be a next time round, there was some debate as to that – they'd specialise. Not in terms of genre – that was crass – but in terms of period.

That night, they opened up, they shared their dreams. In turn, they fantasised about putting their knowledge into words or owning record shops; but, like when they were young, they only ever fantasised about it. Although they now had the talent and the financial clout to make it happen, they didn't want to be involved. Partly this was because it would break the rules of their friendship, but mostly it was because they realised they were still what they'd always been – they were fans. It was for this reason that none of them – excepting Ray's brief flirtation – had ever pursued the performing side: they didn't want to be stars, they wanted to have stars. In the same way that, by and large, folk don't want to be Gods, folk want to worship Gods.

And so things continued.

Until, that was, the evening one month short of the third anniversary of their first meeting.

Hilly didn't turn up.

Hilly was never late. He'd never been late for anything in his life. He just didn't do things like that.

Martin and Ray waited. They didn't start. They wouldn't start without Hilly.

After about an hour, the phone rang. It was a guy who introduced himself as being Phil, Hilly's brother-in-law.

There'd been an accident, Phil said, Hilly had been involved in an accident up at his work.

It seemed important for Phil to take his time and explain as best he could everything that had happened.

It was ten days ago. Hilly had been doing a flitting over the old town. They'd been taking a chest-freezer down a flight of stairs when the guy at the top end had lost his grip. While the guy endeavoured to retrieve his grip, Hilly had tried to wedge the chest-freezer against the bannister. But, somehow, the chest-freezer slipped, pushing Hilly down the stairs.

Phil said he wasn't sure what had happened after that, but next thing anybody knew was that Hilly was flat out at the foot of the stairs. He must've lost his footing or something because the chest-freezer hadn't moved. It had stayed put, perfectly wedged between the bannister and the wall.

Ray asked if Hilly was alright.

Phil took a deep breath. No, he said, Hilly wasn't alright. Hilly was in a coma. He'd been unconscious for ten days.

As much as Ray had been half-expecting something like that, the actual words still managed to shock him in a way that amounted to nothing less than physical pain.

Ray asked when they could go up and visit. Phil said whenever, they could come up any time they wanted.

Ray thanked Phil for letting them know, and said they'd probably be up later on.

Ray told Martin. They talked about what they should do.

They were both thinking along the same lines, but they didn't want to do it – they didn't want to make a tape up for Hilly.

It seemed corny. It seemed sick. It seemed like interfering.

But the more they went on about it, the more it made sense. Really, it was the only thing they could do. That was what this night was all about. The records were more important to Hilly than Martin and Ray ever were. Hilly was the one who always said he'd rather be blind than deaf. It was one of those challenges he always set the other two, like a childhood dare – would you rather be blind or deaf?

The deciding factor was when they got round to thinking about what would've happened if the circumstances had been reversed. It's what Hilly would've done. Hilly wouldn't even have thought about it, he'd just have gone ahead and done it.

Ray looked out the list of Hilly's all-time favourite records. They used that as their guide to make the tape up.

It proved to be a truly horrible experience, listening to all these records, records that would normally have got them so excited, records, as Hilly put it, that made them feel so alive. After a while, they turned the sound as low as they could get away with, and busied themselves doing other things. Martin made a few calls, Ray went for petrol.

Even so, the process, by its very nature, could not be speeded up, and once they'd filled a side of a C-90, they called it a day, and headed up to the hospital.

They always said that the thing about folk in these situations was how normal they looked, how peaceful, but Hilly didn't look normal. He didn't look pained or distressed or harmed in any way, but in no way could you have said he looked normal.

There were four visitors already sitting round the bed.

Other than to say hello, Martin and Ray hadn't spoken to Hilly's mum for close on ten years, but she acknowledged them as though she'd only just seen them the day before. The passing of so much time didn't seem to mean anything.

A bloke stood up and offered his hand. He introduced himself as being Phil, Hilly's brother-in-law, the guy that had phoned. Phil introduced the two women sitting by the bedside as being his sisters, Sarah and Julie. A second later he added that Sarah was Hilly's wife. Martin and Ray hadn't seen Sarah since the day of the wedding. If they hadn't been told her name, they wouldn't've recognised her.

Phil started to apologise for taking so long to let them know, but stopped when Ray shook his head to indicate that it didn't matter.

Martin took the tape and the Walkman from his bag. He asked if it was okay to leave them. The folk seemed a bit unsure but nobody objected. Martin explained as how the tape was made up of Hilly's favourite records. Everybody looked at Martin as though he was talking some kind of foreign language.

Hilly's mother told Martin just to go ahead. She put her arm around Sarah's shoulder and said, 'You know he loves his music, hen, you know he loves his music.'

Martin switched the machine on. The tinny beat could be heard coming through the earphones.

Ray went over and turned the volume up. It wasn't loud enough. It wouldn't've been loud enough for Hilly.

To look at it, it was like one of those awkward scenes folk always laugh at when they see it on telly. Hilly wouldn't've laughed, of course. Hilly liked a laugh but Hilly hated comedy. He had never seen the point of jokes and if he'd ever laughed at a film or sit-com then there was nobody present when he'd done so. Knowing, he called it. Knowing meaning smart-arse, knowing meaning ironic. But, in practice, it always turned out to be the exact opposite. Folk that knew nothing about nothing pretending they did.

Soon, Martin and Ray were beginning to feel distinctly uncomfortable. Not for themselves but for Hilly's family. They felt they didn't belong. They didn't know these people. The only person they knew was the one on the bed, and, at this precise moment in time, they felt as though they'd never really known him at all. They felt as though they'd only ever met him.

Martin took the initiative. He suggested that maybe they should come back later. Ray agreed. He took out a business card and handed it to Sarah, telling her that if ever she was needing any help with anything, anything at all, then just to get in touch. He said it again just to make sure she understood that he meant it.

Martin and Ray left the hospital. Without so much as a word, they drove out to the docks. They didn't want to be indoors, in any kind of home.

It was no wonder that at times like this folk had a habit of turning religious. There were no rules telling them how to behave. No precedent that told them how they should feel. Everything they felt was wrong. Guilt. Regret. Shame. Fear.

And, most of all, anger.

They started flinging stones and rocks out into the water, burning off their energy. This was the worst night of their lives, and it was compounded by the near ridiculous image of Hilly's family sitting round his bed watching him listening to a Walkman.

These people didn't understand.

Or, then again, maybe it was Martin and Ray who didn't understand.

See that was the problem. Their Tuesday nights were tantamount to a secret. And folk liked secrets. Its very success had to do not only with the way they avoided bringing up their problems, but the way it all had nothing to do with anybody else.

That was how no one had got in touch with them. Nobody knew about them. Nobody knew what went on. Hilly would never've mentioned these nights to anybody. Sure, okay, he probably said he was going round to see friends and play records, but he'd never've told anybody about what went on. Martin and Ray didn't, and if they didn't then there was no way Hilly would've. You could only talk to folk about such things, your passions, when they would understand, and nobody they knew, nobody Hilly would know, would understand all this.

For no real reason they could think of other than they wanted to, Martin and Ray decided to head back up to the hospital.

They'd leave it a while, though. They wanted privacy. They wanted their secrecy.

They went back to Ray's and made up more tapes. They taped records from Hilly's list, records from their own lists that Hilly had regretted not including in his own, and the records they'd intended playing that night. This time, they taped with the sound up. They were positive about what they were doing. They were doing what it made sense for them to do. The only thing they could do. It was what they'd done for the first Tuesday of every month for the past three years and it was what they were going to do now.

When they were ready, they returned to the hospital.

Sarah was still there, still sitting by Hilly's bedside.

She explained as how one of them always stayed over and slept on a Parker Knoll in an adjoining room. She didn't seem as wary as she'd done earlier. Truth be told, she looked too tired to be bothered. The Walkman lay on the bedside table, the earphones by its side.

Martin put the new tape in the machine. He fitted the earphones on Hilly, then switched it on.

It was Ray who broke the silence. There were things that needed to be explained.

'You don't know anything about us, do you?' he said.

Sarah shook her head.

'It's a long story,' said Martin.

And, since there was nothing else to do, they told her the story: about how they first met; how they always fell out; their nights playing records.

When they finished Ray laughed. 'Do you realise,' he said, 'this is the first time we've ever talked about him and not slagged him off?'

The three looked over at Hilly. The music stopped. Ray

switched the tape over. He turned the volume up a bit then closed the curtain round the bed.

Sarah told the story of how she met up with Hilly. It was a familiar story. The courtship was so typically Hilly, so single-minded, so matter-of-fact.

Just as Sarah was going on to explain what plans she and Hilly had been making for the future, the curtain round the bed was pulled back.

It was the doctor. 'Do you think you could maybe turn that down, please?' she said. 'It carries, you know.'

Martin apologised. He explained what they were doing.

'Still,' said the doctor, 'it's past one o'clock in the morning.'

Martin went over. He turned down the music.

The doctor tickled Hilly's toes then made a note on her clipboard. 'Are you alright?' she said to Sarah. 'Do you not think that maybe you should get some rest?'

Sarah looked at the other two.

'On you go,' said Martin. 'We'll stay here.'

'Are you sure?' said Sarah.

Martin and Ray nodded. They weren't going anywhere. The doctor smiled a thank you as she led Sarah away into a tiny side-room.

Alone at last, Martin and Ray looked at each other. Then at Hilly. They'd done all they could. They'd played his favourite records, they'd played the ones he'd regretted not having on his list, and they'd played the ones they'd intended playing that night. It was pathetic. Here they were, grown men, successful men, yet this was all they could think to do. Because of Hilly they'd changed so much, so much for the better, but now, when it was most needed, there was nothing they could do in return.

Martin took a piece of paper from his pocket. It was the list of Hilly's favourite records.

Martin studied it. He wasn't staring at it, he was studying it.

If there was an answer, if there was something that could be done, then this was where they'd find it.

After about five minutes Martin reached over and switched off the Walkman. He removed the earphones and placed them and the machine on the bedside cabinet.

Martin continued to study the piece of paper. A further five minutes passed before he finally spoke.

'I think you're wrong,' he said. 'I think you're wrong. And I'll tell you why I think you're wrong. No, listen, listen, you've had your say. See . . .'

Martin went through the list, talking about what they always talked about, the records. Ray pushed up his sleeves and joined in.

They talked about nothing other than records, slagging off the things they always slagged off, going on about the things they always went on about, how important it all was to them. *This* was what it was normally like. Tuesday nights, the three of them together, talking, talking only about records.

Before anybody knew it, it was four o'clock in the morning. They'd been going on like this for the best part of three hours when the doctor returned with another doctor. It was the change of shift, the handover.

The doctor tickled Hilly's toes.

She tickled Hilly's toes again.

She leaned over and shook Hilly by the shoulder. Gently at first, then quite vigorously.

'Can you hear me?' she said.

Hilly moved his lips. He didn't say anything but he moved his lips.

Martin went through and got Sarah. By the time they returned Hilly seemed less peaceful, more restless, almost groggy. For the first time, he looked to be genuinely ill and everybody seemed pleased.

Within the half hour, Hilly was sitting up, taking some fluids and responding to the doctor's questions. He was a bit doped and sluggish but, other than that, there didn't seem to be anything much wrong with him.

Hilly took it all in. Yes, he knew who he was. Yes, he remembered what had happened. Yes, he understood that he was in hospital.

In fact, waking up in hospital didn't seem to bother Hilly – whereas the sight of Martin and Ray did. 'I just had this crazy dream about you pair,' he said. 'Going on and on. Havering the biggest pile of nonsense I've ever heard.'

Martin and Ray smiled, but it was Sarah who laughed. 'Then you could maybe introduce us all some time,' she said.

Hilly turned his head away. The very thought seemed to cause him nothing but shame.

It was then that he noticed the Walkman.

Hilly reached over. He picked up the tapes and the piece of paper.

'Your favourite records,' said Ray.

'We taped them for you,' said Martin.

Hilly seemed chuffed. 'So this is what brought me round then, eh?'

Martin and Ray nodded. Although, as they did so, they were thinking to themselves as how it wasn't the tapes, the music, that had brought Hilly round – no, if anything was responsible, it was them, the sound of their voices. Not that they'd ever dare dream of telling Hilly that, of course. After all, the three friends had an arrangement to keep: they'd only ever meet up on the first Tuesday of the month, and they'd only ever talk about records.

After the Vision

ALAN WARNER

AFTER THE VISION Scorgie lay his forehead against the cold glass of the bus window. A huge bank of sparrows pressed against the road-side hedge then twisted up out of sight above the bus-roof. Scorgie's head and eyes rolled after the flock and he was smiling. An un-realistic scarecrow made from fertiliser bags was between two outstretched orange gloves in a delved field.

Thats me, muttered Scorgie, nodding through the glass past the two guys sat opposite. Both of them glanced at Scorgie.

Been at the Vision? goes Scorgie.

Aye, the wee one went.

What do yous do?

Eh?

What do yous do for a living?

Painter and decorator; he's with BT.

Aye? I'm a salvager. A diver. Do you understand?

Aye. Sort of offshore like?

Nah, away. Away in one of the far places. So what DJ did yous like best?

The Angel, they both nodded.

Aye he's good the Angel. On your own, just the two of yous?

Yup.

I've a team myself but theyre at home. Praying.

There was no talking after this but Scorgie kept staring at them. Scorgie says, I hope yous werent on anything boys. Me? I never take anything. This is cause I am a maniac.

The bus was swinging into the station forecourt. The boys didnt say a thing.

Scorgie says, See all the stones, all the standing stones in all the rigs and policies? Those standing stones were waiting for Jesus. He's the only ecstasy we need.

Scorgie stood up and got off the bus. Inside the railway station the two lads saw Scorgie get on the train for the capital so they both walked over to the bar.

Scorgie sat opposite an oil rigger from the flare-offs to the east. The rigger pestered Scorgie to play cards. When Scorgie had lost five pounds he moved to a toilet and locked himself in. He sat on the toilet seat with his face in his hands till the train got to the capital. He changed trains. Cause he hadnt slept for two nights he got shaken awake by the guard in the city where a branchline heads to the north.

Out in the evening streets Scorgie began to walk through the city. Some younger passersby looked at the clothes he was wearing: trainers caked in mud, shiny Puma tracksuit bottoms, a shirt that seemed to be made of silver foil and hung over it an orange spongy-looking top with a zipper. It was a diver's wet suit jacket.

When Scorgie reached 194 Woodlands Road he walked into the dark of a close then leaped the stairs two at a time to the greeny light coming through the roof glass up the top landing. He knocked on the door to the right with the swastika painted on it. The door didnt open. Scorgie knocked again. He cooried down and poked in the letterbox. Windows within the flat must have been open cause a soft rush of air pushed against his eyes. Scorgie's eyelids fluttered a moment then he coo-ed into the letterbox. Then he shouted: BURN YOUR LEATHERS TOWNIES!

The volume of the shout echoed down the stairs. Scorgie straightened up then he ambled back down the stairs and out in the dusk light. He squinted up and down the pavement then began walking. When he came to a grocers he went in and bought a pen. Embossed on the side was:

SCOTLAND

Scorgie left the grocers and scrutinized the streets. Pieces of paper were skittering about with layers of dust. He leaned and picked up a Burger King receipt. He climbed back up to the door.

Scorgie had to lean against the door and scribble vigorously with the pen to get it going then under a squiggle he wrote:

I'm a friend of Hacker's. He says he crashes here when he's using the university computers and it would be okay for me to crash. I've missed my last train. I'll call back later, say 8ish. Hope yous arent out all night or I'll be on these city streets.

Scorgie   6:30

He was about to pop this note through the letterbox then hesitated. There was a drawing pin among old pin holes stuck in the brownish-coloured wood of the door. The drawing pin was covered with a smear of the swastika's white paint. Scorgie tried to pick the drawing pin free with his flat, worn down thumb nail. Then he tried to tug it out using the strap buckle on his big diving watch but the pin wouldnt budge.

Scorgie snapped his fingers. From within the wet suit jacket he took out a small plastic comb and drew it through his hair a few times. He snapped one of the long teeth off the comb. Using one of the old pin holes he fixed the note to the door with the comb tooth.

Back down the stairs Scorgie began walking till he was beyond the university lands. To pass the time he had a half pint and whisky in every pub he passed. He took on ballast in The Doublet, Studio One, Tennents Bar, The Aragon, The Two Ways, The Argyll, The Caernarvon, The Halt, then he climbed back up to the door and knocked. The note was still there and there was no reply. Scorgie hissed out loud and sauntered out under the night. Again he crossed the university lands and was part way down a thorough-fare when he ran into a guy called Duffles. They had once spent a summer working on the forestry near the isthmus away in the far places.

Duffles! Fucks sake man what brings you to the B.B. City?

The guy gave Scorgie a stoner gaze, nodded and says, I work here now.

Cmon I'll get us a pint in, goes Scorgie.

They settled in the Aragon with a Guinness each. Scorgie asked after Duffles' mother and sister but he hadnt been home for over a year. Duffles says, Its all fucking townies and new folk moving up; all the young Mullochs are just reduced to caravans. Anyway I've important work to do here.

Aye, what is it youre working at? Scorgie says.

Well I work up beyond the university lands at the big crematorium theyve there.

A crematorium. Whats it like there then? went Scorgie.

Oh its good. Its magic. Pays okay, better than when we were snedding and cubing with the commission.

Aye that was utter shite, goes Scorgie.

Duffles says, I've a room in a flat with two townie fellows; good lads they are, cracks brilliant.

Aye? Look Duffles I'm a bit stuck. I've missed the ten past six train, I've been away in the back of beyond at the Vision. Would there be any chance of us crashing at yours for the night?

No bother, shrugged Duffles.

Oh grand. Thats great I was told to stay over at this address but theres no a soul about and I'd visions of me wandering the streets all night. I'm pretty mortal but lets get another couple in, went Scorgie and he crossed to the bar. When he came back with the nips Duffles was rolling a tiny wee cigarette.

I heard about your father Scorgie and I'm sorry, says Duffles.

Aye well it was the fucking bank hounding him till they drove him demented; its those merchants in the temple I wont forgive, goes Scorgie.

Have you got the farm now?

Naw naw, I'm building my own place at The New Projects, right down on the point where I've got the boat and a compressor up by the house. I gave most of my money to the sister with her having the kids and that.

Duffles says, You shouldnt despair. I know it mustve been a shocker but he's in a better place.

Scorgie took a swallow and went, Thats what I believe. I never took you for a religious person, Duffles.

Well, looks can deceive, he goes.

How long have you been down here now? says Scorgie.

Duffles thought hard on this then went, A few years now it'll be, a *good* few years.

Duffles gave the stoner gaze again.

What is it you do out at the crematorium? asked Scorgie.

I'm The Incinerator.

What?

I'm The Incinerator. I control the gas taps and monitor the temperatures in the furnace, says Duffles.

Right enough, youre the man then, eh, goes Scorgie.

There was a gap in the conversation then Duffles went, You see them burning y'know.

What, do you have cameras in there or something?

No, no, the coffins come through on the conveyor so I have a big observation window made of insulated glass right in front of my operating position. I *see* them burning away right in front of my nose.

What you see everything?

Oh aye, you have to. I have to ensure everything is completely incinerated – the bones and that. Its my job, to, quote, 'confirm remains are minimal'. Dont want any lumps in the urn.

So you see it all as it happens through the window?

Oh aye.

I mean . . . whats it fucking like? says Scorgie.

Duffles was silent a while then goes, I initiate the burners and the coffins flare up really quickly. The coffin lining comes flapping out cause the extractor suction is strong in there. The fabric just shoots up and combusts instantly. Then *they* start – the bodies. Usually the coffin has pretty much protected them so you see them unharmed at that point when I increase the temperature. See, the manager likes me to economise on the gas so you burn away the coffin at a lower temperature – in fact we're going to start recycling the coffins soon. After the coffin's burned away and you get to them – the bodies – well then you can really crank on the fucking heat.

Scorgie says, Jesus, it sounds pretty heavy, I mean day in day out you must do plenty . . . eh bodies. Talking personally, I believe that would get to me eventually. I believe in the afterlife but our mortality must be so obvious seeing what you see.

Duffles shook his head slowly, No man, no way, its not like that at all; thats what I felt in the beginning but now, now I've never felt *so* religious before. I've never believed in the afterlife so much as now, seeing the beautiful things I've seen. My mates from the flat feel the same.

What, do they work there too? goes Scorgie.

Duffles goes, No, no. Mid-week my mates come up to the incinerator room with me and we pull this big long bench up in front of the observation window. We've some real good tabs up the flat, over seventy trips, so we all of us drop a good scoop of it then when the rushes start, Weeeee, I open the metal shutter and we just watch all day . . . I mean they all burn in such different ways when I crank up the heat. Some just lie there and smoke away in a boring old pyre but others, *especially* the younger ones, are spectacular . . . like a revelation man. You see, in that kind of temperature-increase, combustion can take place all over the body: in the thighs, or in the breasts or especially inside the skull. Some of them man, their spines will curl up in the heat so they sit straight up in front of you, their hair and their eyebrows bubble up instantly and then their clothes start to burn and get torn off in the updraft so you see them naked, sometimes lovely young girls and that . . . then these fucking jets of flame are coming out the fucking eye-sockets man and the lips just melt away with sparks and flames fucking spewing out through the gritted teeth then the whole fucking head just explodes man, fucking explodes, fucking flames devouring everything and we're all sat there tripping out our faces going, Ahh fuck LOOK AT THAT!

Scorgie mumbled, Well, it sure beats afternoon television.

Duffles had hardly touched his Guinness or nip. Scorgie looked at him and says, Duffles, no think you should steady the buffs on the tabs, you know, in your line of work. I mean I can see youre pretty motivated but you dont want to start getting too involved.

Duffles went, I've been taking lots of photos.

Photos?

Aye, I spend all my money on tabs and film man, I develop it in the darkroom we've built at the flat. I've some cracking shots. I'm using a Nikon F4 and a SB25 flash up on a tripod. I've got boxes of prints at the flat you'll see tonight.

Ah, Duffles what I think I'll do is just try those other folk once more and if they're not there I'll make my way over to your place. How does that sound?

Whatever, but you've go to lie back and check out some of these photos, there's one of this young girl, says Duffles fiddling madly with another roll up.

Right, eh jot your address down on a beer mat and I'll be off, goes Scorgie pulling out the SCOTLAND pen.

As Duffles wrote down his address, really leaning into the paper, he was saying, I see it all so clearly now, everything so simple. So much work to be done. Sometimes when I'm just sat in a pub looking at people I can see flames in their eyes and when they hold back their heads to laugh I can see this red glow in past their fillings . . .

It was the last thing Scorgie heard him say as he lurched up grabbing the beer mat saying, Right Duffles, if I dont find those folk in I'll see you soon. If I'm no round maybe see you back home, you should try a break.

Outside Scorgie swayed to one side, gritted his teeth, says, Fucks sake, and tossed the beer mat onto the pavement.

He walked quickly looking back twice then crossed over the university lands again till he came to 194 Woodlands Road. There was nobody in. Scorgie trotted back down the stair and out into the streets. Up near the top of the road there was a chip shop and cause he noticed he was famished he stood in the queue looking at the floor and shaking his head a couple times. There was a display of a supposed sea bed through a glass panel along the front of the counter. There were shells, plastic starfish and a strange coloured plastic plaice – Scorgie stared at it when the girl behind the counter says, Yes?

Salt and vinegar please, goes Scorgie.

Eh? went the girl.

Salt and vinegar.

What *on*? shouts the girl.

Oh, sorry, eh a fish tea please, says Scorgie.

Eh?

No. I'll have a Mars Bar supper.

A Mars Bar supper?

Aye.

Outside with his Mars Bar supper, Scorgie walked hunched over it, lifting portions out the brown paper and up to his mouth. After eating less than half the food he flung the whole thing in a bin while walking on, rubbing his fingers up and down the wet suit sleeves.

He walked into the first place he came to. It was a sort of wine bar place. He ordered a Guinness, put it down on a table near the toilets and went in for a slash. Back in the bar he stood by a pillar with the glass tipped to his mouth as he nuzzled away at the head of froth. A few folk looked over at him while he drained the pint. He zipped up the jacket hiding the silver shirt then took his glass back up and ordered another pint. When he got back to the pillar he didn't touch the full pint but left it sat on the table where he could reach it. Scorgie stood for a bit holding his chin pressed down into his collar bone and he burped out.

His face got very pale then Scorgie slapped his hand up to his mouth to stop the two jets of vomit shooting out his nostrils. He reached the Gentlemens in one step, shouldered in the outer door and another step took him to the cubicle door, leant slightly forward . . .

ENGAGED

Scorgie booted the cubicle door with a deft clip at the same time dropping his hands allowing the clods of spew to burst out all over the bare thighs of the startled looking big guy sat on the toilet having a dump.

Scorgie tried to turn the jet of orangey-coloured gadge away from the shouting man but it splattered off the cubicle partition with little yellow shards of some vegetable matter settling in the guy's hair. Scorgie took one gasp of breath then as the big guy with his trousers about his feet began to rise, Scorgie punched him as violently as he could, on the nose. Scorgie felt the bridge bone pulverise and slide sideways against his ring and the big fellow's back hit against the cistern knocking the enamel top out of place. The guy sat back in the seat, head forwards and dark blood started pattering onto the hairy thighs.

Scorgie spat on the floor and says, Oh, jesus I'm sorry pal, but I mean who has a shite in a pub?

Once out and walking quick up the road, Scorgie looked down where the sharp pain on his finger was. The punch had driven the gold ring with the image of Saint Columba into his flesh. He shook the hand and says, Oh remorse.

Scorgie took a right into a less busy street then left into another. At the far end he came out on a busy boulevard that he knew as The Great Road.

Over by the row of concrete traffic bollards two young women were arguing with an older man who was wearing a bright pullover pulled tight over his paunch. Scorgie closed his eyes and opened them. Tears of affection for the man gave diamonds on the streetlamps.

Just some simple photos. All the gear's up the house, says the guy.

No way, cause what comes next? went the taller of the girls, then she lifted a lemonade bottle to her mouth.

Thats up to yous girls and how much of a buzz yous like out life.

If you dont mind me saying so pal, youre a perv, goes the other girl.

Hey, hear this? He's trying to take us up his flat to take scuddy photos of us, the taller girl bawled at Scorgie, looking over at him.

Aye? Its a city of photographers this, went Scorgie, moving closer to the group.

Thats some clothes youve got on there.

Thats real class that is, real class, says the plumper of the two girls.

Scorgie nodded and goes, I've been in the back of beyond away at a rave.

The Vision? Jay and I like Soul, eh?

Aye: STOP IN THE NAME OF, the two girls started singing out of time and throwing their arms round each other.

Want a blast? goes the smaller girl waving the bottle that she was holding.

Scorgie tipped the bottle right back then stepped in a circle to spit a mouthful back onto the pavement where it fizzed busily on the concrete.

Hoi, thats a right waste that.

I thought it was only juice.

You must be joking. Do you no drink or something?

Too right, I've just chugged up and I'm parched, says Scorgie.

Jay, Jay hear this? The boy's just chugged up.

Thats a shame this early.

I'm dying to get a sleep, I've been up two nights but I'm locked out this flat on Woodlands Road, went Scorgie.

Aye? we're locked out too. We're meant to be up in that flat there with our pal McLayley whos having his wee party.

A party? I bet I could lie down there somewhere; no one's really going to notice eh?

Well McLayley probably wouldnt mind. Renee, McLayley wouldnt mind if this boy had a wee sleep in his flat eh?

I can pay him in some gear, I've got some tabs on me, went Scorgie.

McLayley would be into that but we cant get in, the skinnier girl nodded to the tenement corner.

Have you tried going up? If its a party probably no one can hear yous.

Naw, its just me, Renee and McLayley'll be at the party but he doesn't seem to be in, we've buzzed and buzzed.

Renee goes, He'll be over at the union for the student happy hour. He'll be over there.

Thats a three mile walk, went Jay.

What in the university lands? says Scorgie.

Naw, no this uni, the *other*.

The *other*? goes Scorgie.

Renee started singing a song. It wasnt a soul song and she was waving the bottle about so it fizzed up a paler colour inside.

Shush, shush, went Jay.

Sing a decent song, the sash or something, says the older man.

Renee changed to another song. The only words Scorgie could make out were the chorus where I.R.A. was repeated again and again.

Going to shush, says Jay and Renee shut up.

Hey, hey Jacques Cousteau. I was talking to the girls here, says the guy in the pullover holding his hands out to Scorgie in appeal.

Jacques Cousteau! screamed Renee and both the girls took hysterics of giggles. The girls were bending forwards and backwards in their laughs so's the two men faced each other across them. Scorgie smiled at the man.

I dont reckon you can handle it, Scorgie says quietly.

What? went the guy.

I dont believe you can handle it, I dont reckon you can mount the blood-red horse of strife and stay on it.

What? goes the guy.

And to him that sat upon it there was given to take peace from the earth, and to bring it about that men should slay each other, and a great sword was given to him. Revelation Six, says Scorgie.

The guy shook his head and chuckled. Scorgie lifted the broken skin of his finger up to his mouth and he started licking the blood round the cold metal.

We're away with Jacques Cousteau, shouted Renee, grabbing Scorgie by the arm and twisting him round.

Scorgie looked back and the guy in the pullover put his hands in his pockets and started shouting, Yous are losers girls, losers do you hear, yous are going nowhere, *nowhere*!

Away and fuck pervy, shouted Renee not looking back.

Jay had linked the other arm of Scorgie and it was when they were in motion it became clear to him how utterly mortal both the girls were. They advanced in a way that was partly pulling him and partly falling, the different weights of the tall and short girl along with the erratic steps, pivoted Scorgie from side to side while they kept up a non-stop spray of conversation.

They were moving up the wide pavement forcing other parties of folk coming the other way, to step aside.

Hey Jacques Cousteau, our mate's called McLayley McLayley and we're off to find him.

Thats right.

McLayley McLayley?

Thats right.

Where you from Jacques Cousteau?

From one of the far places.

Here, went Renee and she dunted the end of the bottle against Scorgie's teeth. He pretended to drink then handed the mix of whisky and Irn Bru back.

Renee started singing another song and passing groups of boys seemed to be jeering at the three of them.

Shut it, youre going to get us our teeth kicked in, says Jay.

The three of them had reached a network of traffic islands, spiral pedestrian bridges and a mass of headlights flowing beneath them into the sodium lamps of an underpass. Renee took a last slug of the bottle then flung it into the alcove of an emergency exit to some building. The glass exploded out across the pavement and Scorgie glanced around.

They crossed the roads and were at the bottom of a main street with Renee singing as they moved through the lights. Outside a bar called Oceans Eleven Renee says, Thats the place for you Jacques.

Let's set sail then, goes Scorgie.

Press on, went Jay.

Renee started singing again and a girl coming out of Oceans Eleven snapped, Going to shut up you pape cow.

Renee tried to tug free but Scorgie jerked her back and the guy that was with the girl was tugging her saying, Her brothers in the army in Belfast for fuck sake.

Sorry pal, she's steaming, goes Scorgie and the guy nodded and walked away pulling the girl with him.

You'd better cool it on the sectarian top ten, went Scorgie.

I'm bursting to pee, shouted Renee. She looked up above the glass doorway they were adjacent to. It was a long sheet glass frontage with books and leaflets in the window, a pillar painted a buff colour was before the doorway then another long glass section continued. Renee read out the words above the door.

Centre for Contemporary Arts. Here you stand there Jacques Cousteau and you get there, hen, says Renee. Scorgie stood in the gap to the left of the pillar, Jay to the right. Renee started undoing her jeans and tugging them down.

Fucks sake Renee, goes Jay.

Scorgie coughed and turned round to look out across the wide street. Even though Scorgie's height threw a shadow on Renee where she was cooried down on her hunkers, by looking through either side of the glass corners anybody could see in.

A gang of about ten lads appeared.

Jesus boys, look at this.

Evening gentlemen, says Scorgie.

Ha, ha, for fucks sake, says a lad pushing his head round Scorgie's side. When Scorgie tried to position himself in the guy's view it allowed two other wee fellows to take up a viewing position to his other side.

Hi, fuck off! Renee shouted behind Scorgie.

One lad shouted, Here is the weather forecast, fucking golden showers on Sauchiehall Street.

Jay was shoving two guys back, snarling, Thats my fucking mate you weasely wank.

Are you waiting for a shite or something darling? says one guy to Jay's face and dodged out her way, laughing.

Look at the bush on it, pointed another lad and then Scorgie could hear the tinkle of Renee's belt as she mustve been pulling up her jeans.

Oh, for fucks sake! a guy moaned and he lifted one of his slip-on moccasins. There was a sucking sound. Scorgie looked down: a large flood of Renee's dark pish-liquid was running in different streams round and under the guy's shoes then spreading in rivulets across the slope of the wide pavement, wiggling a route through a summer's dust and into the gutter.

All the guys jamp back and started scraping their footwear on the pavement and muttering. There was a complete puddle round Scorgie's trainers. He turned, saw Renee fiddling with her belt buckle and he stepped out onto the pavement.

Look at your man here, one guy says.

Yons a fucking diving suit he's on.

Hi, you'd need a diving suit with her about.

Jay was waving at Scorgie from further up the road, Hih Renee cmon, *come* on.

Scorgie took Renee by the arm and tried to lead her on up the road but she stepped in front of him and spoke in a low voice, Jacques Cousteau, I think you're real class; then she pulled his head down on her lifted-up mouth. Her tongue moved in, behind Scorgie's teeth and jumped about. She was grinding Scorgie's face onto hers by pulling and massaging at the back of his neck with her long gold-ringed fingers. Neck hairs of Scorgies kept getting snapped on the rings and their roots pinged. He could hear the big crowd of lads all cheering as he kissed on, just wanting to close his eyes and sleep. Right there leaned on the plate of Renee's face and her long body against him; though he could feel through her pullover the shiny material of the slip she'd on under, Scorgie just wanted to sleep, to dangle down onto the pavement. Sleep.

Renee pulled back and looked down at her feet taking a breath.

Is she too much for you pal? shouted one of the boys. Renee began shifting and snogging at him again then Jay was pulling them apart and the three of them were leaving the shouting boys behind. They were walking on, not talking till Jay says, We mustve walked for miles.

Groups of people were moving in the opposite direction eating out of take-away food packages that steam was rising from.

I'm starving, goes Jay.

We've got to follow the yellow brick road to the union where we'll find McLayley McLayley, Renee told them.

They had crossed the university lands and moved through the sunken street where clots of night people were walking erect down the feeder lanes onto the main drag. Groups of suited men gathered round tight dressed girls with electric hair; a million pieces of jewellery were picking up the busy movements of cabs and buses then the three turned from the noise and light into a deserted concrete courtyard. A tall brick hall with needle-thin window strips that changed colour to a repeating beat was over the way. They un-linked hands and climbed the wide apron of low steps to a row of about twenty doors. They began trying to push or pull one of them open while a guy at a desk inside watched them curiously.

Aha! goes Jay and she disappeared inside. Renee and Scorgie followed.

Do you know McLayley McLayley, says Jay to the guy at the desk.

McLayley who?

McLayley McLayley.

McLayley McLayley?

Aye.

No.

We're here to see if he's up the stair. We cant find him.

Have you got your matric cards?

Hah, we're not students, neither's McLayley McLayley but he used to be and he comes here with friends that sign him in. If I could just go up for a wee look?

I cant let you in without a card.

Ah, just for a wee look.

Scorgie says, The lassie just wants to check if he's there and she's gone; we've nowhere to stay tonight less we find this guy.

Look its just shutting up there, strict license, we've already lost it twice so they chuck everyone out in ten minutes, no exceptions.

What is it you study pal? goes Scorgie.

Pardon?

Do you study computer science?

No.

Scorgie nodded at the guy then says, Cmon, we'll wait outside.

Renee sat on the steps with her legs amazingly wide apart. She vomited repeatedly onto the concrete. She spat a few times then moved along the steps and sat a good way from where she'd done the sicking up. She gripped her legs and tugged them up to her.

Scorgie was lying on his back looking up into the orangey sky turning above him. He'd sat up for a moment to watch the process of Renee throwing up then he'd lain back again.

Who *is* your friend McLayley McLayley?

Jay, standing over him smoking a cigarette says, He's just this nutter, he's funny, all these terrible things happen to him. He's a dropout from everything. He lives in that flat with his wee doggy Ratto.

Where do you and Renee live?

Way out on The Orbital.

The Orbital?

Aye.

If we dont find this McLayley McLayley can I come back and crash at yours?

Jay shrugged, Dont know what Mum'll say.

I could always go to a club but if I fall asleep they'll chuck me out. My train's no till eight and I've got all these tabs on me.

Just take them, that'll keep you awake.

Ah, not me. I dont take drugs anymore.

Isnt that all you do. At your Visions?

Not me, I'm praying and thinking all the time. They're great places to go for a praying. We all used to go, me and my friends, my team doing our praying and thinking, this was years back when it was all underground but we dont go anymore, we're saving our money for The Big One.

The big one? goes Jay.

Aye. The Big One.

We dont know what The Big One is ourselves but we all know its coming, coming soon . . . My father . . . died three years ago, I'd taken some tabs and sleeping pills, I went off the end of the world and I never came back, I travelled to a strange place, I couldnt remember how I got there. I'd wandered out beyond the concession lands, I had all these visions, thought I was getting chased by black helicopters and I was mortally terrified of trees . . . Scorgie's voice, hoarse and monotonous filled in the collage of traffic noise then merged with the babble of folk pouring out the rows of doors. The groups of people moved down the stairs and walked round Scorgie's stretched-out-body.

Get the state of him. Lucky bastard, a guy says.

Renee and Jay were moving amongst the people looking for McLayley but the clutters of folk moved off under the sodium lights toward DARKTOWN over the buildings.

Nah, the bampot isnt here, goes Renee.

Lets take a fast black to The Great Road, says Jay.

Scorgie stood up and dusted his hands on his arse.

Oh no, Mohammed, goes Renee.

Ah, fuck, went Jay.

Hello all, says Mohammed nodding at Scorgie.

Hello, you seen McLayley at all?

Nah, he's lying low. I saw him last month and he didnt have two pence to rub the gether. Where are we headed then, going on somewhere else?

Aye the Blue Lagoon, says Jay and the four of them began walking separately out the courtyard and further up the hill. They turned into the chippie and since Scorgie didnt want to eat he stood by the window. He noticed how Renee cut in front of Mohammed in the queue. They all ordered chicken suppers.

Breast or leg? the guy behind the counter kept saying. Each time the guy said it Scorgie found himself looking at the pale tops of Jay's bosom showing out of the burgandy-colour print dress then he was peering at the denim legs he'd seen Renee hold so far apart.

Scorgie moved his lips among the hissing and banging of the chip shop. His lips formed a word: then he squeezed his eyes shut.

Jay was served first so she crossed to Scorgie and whispered, Give Mohammed the slip, cmon.

Outside they walked ahead. Jay neatly folded back the paper enfolding the chicken supper. After she'd torn the brown skin aside, her red painted nails flashed among the pure whiteness of the meat she picked at.

Scorgie looked back and Renee came tanking out the Blue Lagoon neon bawling something. Scorgie and Jay ran on with a wall at their sides. There was the loud sound of a train moving underneath the wall. The bright orange beacon of a free fast black swung round. Jay made to step out into the road but Scorgie closed his hand on her arm. A car wheeched by, moving the dress around her shins. Scorgie held out his arm and the taxi brakes squeaked. The driver was pointing as to what way they were headed and should he do a U-turn to their side. Jay pointed up the long, ascending street. The taxi did a U-turn and holding her supper Jay bent down and ducked inside. Scorgie climbed in and sat beside her as the slaps of Renee's feet were outside and puffing, she stooped in and slammed the door.

Quick, quick, The Great Road, goes Jay.

Renee was twisting in the seat looking out the back window so she leaned her weight against Scorgie's side.

The taxi revved forward then slowed and stopped at the first red light. There was an entire grid of traffic lights ahead. As soon as the taxi moved off from the one, they were at the next set turning amber.

Who is that guy? says Scorgie.

Mohammed. He's a real pain. Sort a guy you end saying goodnight to through your letter box.

Why do you call him Mohammed?

Dont know.

The taxi stopped at the following intersection. Renee let out a huff and blew on her chicken then she jumped. The door beside her had clicked open and the long creeper snaked in and put its end down on the taxi carpet. Attached to the rest of the long leg, Mohammed ducked in and settled on one of the fold-down chairs, twisting his legs round so they would fit in along the partition below the driver's back, arched over Scorgie and Jay's feet.

Did yous lose me? Mohammed says and he began eating his chicken supper.

The taxi moved through the intersections and between traffic islands then it cruised up onto an elevated section of highway and down onto The Great Road. There was no speaking. Scorgie looked at Jay: at how her skin was pale, bright red nails and mouth with streaks of black hair fallen down over the white face.

The taxi had stopped at another set of traffic lights. Mohammed was hunched over the ruins of the chicken. Scorgie noticed Jay had leaned forward and was glancing across him at Renee who turned, looking out through the rear window, her side pressing against him. Jay moved her lips and Scorgie frowned.

Renee shouted, NOW!

Jay shoved open her door and with the dress tugged up round her thighs she vanished at a sprint down a darker side street. The right hand door was swinging open and Renee had run across the traffic-free lanes where she was horseing it away.

The taxi driver had spun round clocking what was happening. He opened his door and stepped out. Mohammed was turning his head from one open door to the other, the chicken supper held stiffly under his chin.

Scorgie dived. He toppled himself forward and actually did a dive over the space beside Mohammed, at the same time turning his head to make sure the taxi was up against the left kerb with no possible traffic coming. Scorgie's shoulder thumped the door wide open and his held-out-left hand touched the pavement as he flopped down, half out the taxi, his legs still lying in it. He crawled forward a bit, hands pulling him, rings scratching on the paving stones.

Someone grabbed his fucking foot. Aye for sure, someone had grabbed his foot: Mohammed clinging to Scorgie's cunting trainer. Scorgie booted back his free foot and a chicken supper went flying within the taxi. The driver was in the back, a hold on Mohammed's shoulder with Mohammed gripping Scorgie hanging halfway out the door.

Fucking nutters, nobody does a runner from 187 son, says the cabby.

I cant afford it mister, I cant afford it all on my own, get this guy to chip in, look at the trainers he's on.

'Chips', look at the state of my fucking cab, says the man.

Scorgie sprawled on the pavement caught tight in the grip. A group of folk in dinner suits and long dresses politely passed, glancing a bit at the scene. Scorgie relaxed his leg then gave it the almighty tug – his trainer came off in Mohammed's hand then Scorgie was up and sprinting lopsidedly down the street after Jay, arms held tight to his side, spitting out breaths, increasing speed beside a long row of parked cars, one foot silently landing, the other shoving him on then he swerved round into another street where he saw shadows behind a series of workmen sheds. He stepped off the pavement and in behind one shed he slumped down rocking back and forwards trying to recover breath, then he whispered, Ah fuck it, fuck, fuck, looking down at his sock in the dark. Then he chuckled.

After a few more minutes in the hiding place he came out, looked both ways then began limping along under the street lights, head scope-ing for dog shit on the pavement as he circuited back toward The Great Road.

He heard a hiss, Jacques, Jacques.

He looked over a low privet hedge. Renee and Jay were sat cross-legged.

Get down, Mohammed's about.

Scorgie opened the gate to the garden, the spring squeaked, he closed it gently then kneeled down.

I thought I'd lost yous, whispered Scorgie.

What a cracker, eh? breathed Renee.

Aye it was funny, says Scorgie.

A breeze brushed through the privet.

Does Mohammed know McLayley's flat?

Nah, Mohammed is no allowed to know anyone's address.

If we could get in the close even, theres no way he'd find us, went Scorgie.

Cmon, Jay took him by the hand and they opened the gate and strolled up to the close door. Jay rang a buzzer with:

MCLAYLEY MCLAYLEY

There was no reply. She rang:

AULD/McCRACKEN

Hello, came a voice.

I've a note to post in the top flat for McLayley; could you let me in please, says Jay.

The door buzzed and Scorgie quickly jerked it open.

Away back and get Renee, whispered Jay, but her voice still echoed up the stairs. She put the nib down on the lock.

Outside Scorgie sneaked back into the garden. Renee was asleep, slumped over to one side.

Renee, hoi, hoi, hoi Renee.

Get out of my bedroom, she says.

C'mon we've got in the close, Scorgie threw an arm round her and started trying to pull her up but he sort of slumped down alongside her with his head in the hedge.

Oh Renee, he sighed.

Hey, yous, I've found McLayley, hey yous fucks sake.

A crisp packet was pitter-pattering. It was popping then

jerking. A dried old crisp packet among the twisty roots of the privet hedge. Rain drops hit-hitting the crisp packet next to Scorgie's nose. Scorgie had been sleeping.

Get up, yous are in someone's garden, went Jay.

Scorgie sat up and says, Oh fuck how long have I been here?

Just two minutes, cmon help me up with her.

It's raining its pouring, says Renee when they stood her up. Renee could walk well enough to get back in the close out of the big mild drops coming down. Jay clicked the lock behind them.

Wait and see this Renee, youre no going to believe this.

Scorgie climbed the stairs first, accidentally kicking a doormat.

Jacques, you've only one shoe on.

Aye I know.

They reached the top landing and Jay just opened the door without a key. A small dog yap was heard. They moved into a pitch dark, cluttered hall. The house was lit only by a single candle in the front room. Renee shut the door behind them.

On the middle of the floorboards in the large room a guy was lying on his back. Two eggs were beside his left ear, a puddle of wax on a biscuit tin lid and a low burnt candle by the right.

Renee darling, I've knackered my fucking back.

Whats happened to you?

Sorry yous have been trying to get in I cant move. The doctor came round to see me last night and he boiled me some eggs while he was here. He's getting me in the hospital a week on Wednesday.

A tiny dog with a wagging tail clicked out the kitchen area, mounted the shin of Scorgie's shoeless leg then with his paws wrapped round, pumped away rampantly. Scorgie shook it away.

Well Ratto's got a friend.

This is Jacques. Jacques this is McLayley.

Hello McLayley. What shoe size do you take? says Scorgie, bending over to shake McLayley's uplifted hand as he lay there.

Jacques lost his shoe, says Jay.

Cause of the limited candlelight the standing people were in a near darkness round McLayley's stretched figure.

Cmon, let the dog see the rabbit, form a square circle round me and I'll tell you what happened to me.

Scorgie had noticed an old arm chair behind him so he sat and lay his cheek against the antimacassar breathing in its ancient dustiness. Scorgie took out the four tabs. He tossed them over to McLayley.

I was hoping I could crash for the night, says Scorgie.

No problem, Jacques, thanks. Join me friends? says McLayley placing one each on the tongues of Renee and Jay who were kneeled either side of him as if taking a eucharist as they held their heads back.

McLayley began speaking:

Me and Ratto have been living on porridge for two weeks. Porridge for breakfast, porridge for lunch and porridge with herbs for teatime. I went out Saturday. I had to duck and run past the newsagents cause I'm the only one he orders the *Morning Star* for but I havent been able to afford it for two months.

I went scouting up town to try find this jerk who owes me seventy p. I found the bastard pished, sleeping outside his flat in the flowerbed at Safeways so I frisked the cunt and got a pound twenty six off him. I put the lot on the nose. The three forty five at Cheltenham; Lashing Worthy. Disappeared after the second fence then at the end of the race they announced it was the only one hadn't finished. It'd fallen and been shot on the third.

I was so hungry I was just standing across from William Hills looking in the bakery window at this beautiful fat juicy loaf when there's a tap on my shoulder. I turned round and it was some suit, CID, he says, Ah fucks sake I'm just standing here *looking* man, I says, I'm looking for people fitting your description, he says, Look I dont know what you're on about, I says, Fitting your description to take part in an identity parade. You will be paid five pounds for your services he says, Lead the way, I says and he took me to the police station, then he led me to this cell. I walked in, all these guys and not one of us looks the least bit the same. Most of the lads are fretting cause they have to get off to the match.

Finally the CID in the suit leads us all into this strange room with a long mirror in front of you, spotlights in your face and you must stand in front of this number. I was number 5, and this row of us, eight guys, we're stood there facing our reflections but there's a space between me, number 5 and number 7. Then this guy in handcuffs is led in, they take the cuffs off him and he stands in place 6. I look at him and he glares at me then says, Collaborator. This voice suddenly comes out a speaker FACE THE FRONT 5. So I look straight ahead at my reflection. STOP SMILING 3, the voice goes. Then we hear these lassies' voices on the other side of the mirror and a voice says almost straight away, Five, thats him, number five the fucking bastard. We hear the girl being led out again and the guy beside me is cuffed. We file out and the CID in the suit appears and smacks me on the back, Well done; dont let it bother you, and all the guys laugh. Through the reception we get a fiver each. I rushed over to the bakery and then queued up then says, I want that loaf there, What one? says the girl, That big one there, I says and the girl says, Thats plastic, and everyone in the bakery laughs. I go down to this health shop where they have these leaflets of recipes. I bought all this organic yeast and flour to make my own bread. When I got back here I found the electricity had been cut off. I picked up that armchair to try and throw it across the room and as I hoisted it: crick, I felt my spine go.

The candle sputtered off a bit smoke.

Poor McLayley, says Renee, stroking his forehead.

Will we go out and get you something from the petrol station? says Jay.

Nah, not now youve taken that tab.

You should write down all the stuff that happens to you, says Jay.

I've started doing that. A diary sort of. Not since my back went. There was an old typewriter in the cupboard. The ribbon's awful faint though. I keep making all these mistakes. I can't afford Tippex so I use that bottle of Milk of Magnesia.

My head's really starting to buzz, goes Renee.

Mine too, went McLayley.

Can I go to the toilet? says Scorgie.

Down there on the right.

Scorgie crashed his way through the corridor that seemed to have a ladder lying along it. He stood, breathing in the dark, waiting for his eyes to adjust. There was a shuffling round his legs so he kicked out and yon wee dog scampered away into the candlelight.

There was no lock on the door, he had to kneel to pish straight into the bowl. While he was down there among the slow moving odours, a much-pissed-upon-by-the-males carpet and the toilet bowl sticky with dust and syrupy urine patches he prayed to his Saviour.

Don't hug me to your breast yet; please, give me some more days yet my Lord, Scorgie whispered.

Back in the weak lights of the front room Scorgie found Renee had been blindfolded and she was feeling with her hands along the manky-looking mantelpiece. One of the eggs had been placed on the shelf up to her right. She crossed over into darknesses near the sink. There was a crash and McLayley began roaring with laughter until his back arched and he shouted in pain.

Totally cold, bawled Jay. A plate crashed down and broke clean in two.

Aww, my head, goes McLayley.

Me too, laughed Renee who then walked straight to the egg and started to peel the shell off.

How the fuck did you do that? went Jay. Renee laughed dropping the egg shell pieces on the floor then crossed and pushed the egg slowly into Jay's mouth.

Yes, get the guts up and just do it, whispered McLayley.

Jay sat down and started undoing her boots.

The clothes are coming off now! shouted McLayley then he laughed. The blindfolded girl lifted her jumper and the shiny slip above her head but in such a way as not to tug the blindfold off her face.

Colours have names but there are no names for the colours inbetween, says McLayley. Then after a pause he added, Except Burnt Sienna, and he started laughing.

Renee still had the blindfold and her jeans on but she was crawling in a circular path on the floor chasing one of her shoes that she'd removed. In the shadow her bare breasts hung under her like bats.

Jay had leaned over McLayley and looked into his face. Scorgie watched her hand that was moving on McLayley's leg.

Renee crawled along the side of the lying-down man. Scorgie saw Renee's tongue making stiff little movements into his ear then around McLayley's neck while Jay kissed him full on the mouth and he moved up his hands into her hair. Scorgie smelt smoke and saw Jay making these little sexual thrusts then he noticed, as Jay twisted herself on top of McLayley and was un-doing his shirt buttons that little runt Ratto had pushed in by Jay's thigh where her knee rested. The little dog had joined in, clung round the girl's smooth-looking thigh and pumping away. A shadow crept down the wall but as Scorgie tried to watch, the last fucking candle went out.

Scorgie was curled on the armchair and he'd been listening to the first bird singing. A little light was showing over where the black drapes were pinned above the window.

Though he'd slept through it, the three had produced a mattress from somewhere during the night and they were lying in some odd positions with the man stiffly in the centre beneath a selection of old coats. Scorgie quietly slid down off the chair looking around for the dog. McLayley's trainers were sitting off to the left and Scorgie grabbed with both hands then his legs pushed him up in a sure muscular way to his full height and in two strides he was in the dark hallway. Another stride took him past the toilet and another to the door. Biting his lip he turned the Yale and stepped out onto the landing. He sat on the bottom step and found by crushing down the backs of the trainers and stubbing the toe part down first he could advance forward in an acceptable fashion. Leaving his own trainer at the bottom of the stairs he moved out into the damp morning streets, scraping the trainers along as he went. A thick mist covered The Great Road but a few all-night taxis were still cruising and Scorgie hailed one as its bronze coloured lights appeared. Scorgie double-took on the driver but it was a new face so he swung the door open, got in and told the driver the name of the railway station.

As they moved through the clogged spaces of the streets with the mists stocked up between sandstone buildings the driver started talking:

God said to Saint Peter. Peter I'm going to make a beautiful country. Fertile lowlands, beautiful mountains with graceful waterfalls coming down the sides. Sheltered Glens that glow purple in the summer. I'm going to make the people of this country strong, brave and noble. I'm going to give them a drink that glows like gold, called whisky. This noble country of handsome men and the prettiest girls will be called Scotland. What do you think Peter?

Saint Peter said, Well God that's all very well but do you not think you're being too lavish in the gifts you're bestowing to this country. It sounds like heaven on earth.

God replied to this: Oh there's no possibility of that, wait till you see who I'm going to give them as fucking neighbours!

Scorgie joined the taxi driver's laughs as they pulled into the side of the railway station.

Scorgie had his ticket so he got a table seat and dozed for

a while till the train moved off through the tunnels and into morning sun clearing away the mists.

For three hours west then north the train moved away from the central belt cities into the Far Places. At the military halt, a couple of The Dose brothers sat two seats up from Scorgie. They were from a family of fifteen children including two sets of twins and they were cleaners at the military station. They had two crates of beer with them and they soon started pishing into plastic carrier bags and throwing them out the window at sheep.

Scorgie walked forward.

Aye Aye Scorgie, where have you been?

Never mind where I've been boys I'm trying to rest easy and somehow just your presence is disturbing me, savvy?

We were just having a crack and that.

It's not very nice what you're doing.

Aye, well sorry, we'll move up a bit.

Brilliant idea boys, maybe see yous in the Gluepot one night.

The two Dose brothers moved up the coach into the next one with their beers.

Through The Slip Halt and under the Blackmounts the train moved on. When it stopped at The Falls Platform, the Man Who Walks was stood with a long section of sink top and the actual sink still attached. The Man Who Walks mustve found it in a field. Clods of grass were still stuck to the taps and U-pipe. Molotov the guard wouldnt allow it on the train cause it exceeded length permitted in the Free Baggage Allowance for passengers. Scorgie could hear the argument through the window The Dose brothers had left open.

Man Who Walks leaned the sink unit against the side of the train and delivered it a heavy kick, splitting the unit in the middle. The Man Who Walks threw the draining board section across the wooden platform, hoisted the aluminium sink above his head and stepped onto the train.

The train accelerated on up the pass beyond Five Mile House then into Back Settlement. Whatever The Dose brothers had been up to, Molotov threw them off the train there. They were so drunk they just sat on the gravel platform looking bewildered. As the train pulled out Scorgie gave them an over-enthusiastic wave. They had another six miles to make it home.

Beyond Back Settlement the train slowed through the concession land and around the first of the reed beds. Out on the point Scorgie could see the buildings of The New Projects and just beyond on the higher ground, The Summer Colony.

As the train moved close to the roofs of the bought houses, Scorgie stood up and shuffled to the door. He leaned out, opened the door and got down onto the platform. He slammed the door and stood where he was. The engine blew its horn and a length of exhaust smoke keeled over as it increased its power onto the leaning curve.

Molotov was standing up in the guards' doorway and he nodded and smiled as the train moved by. The moment the end moved past him Scorgie jamp down off the platform. The rails still zinged. Across the track he ducked down through the insect clouds on the Bridle Path. He came out up the road from the Ferry Hotel and walked down to its public bar, The Gluepot.

The barmaid who was known as The Hole of Morar was serving. Scorgie had seen her souped-up black mini with the aerials parked outside.

Aye, Aye.

Hello there. You been away for the weekend?

Yup. Can I have a fresh orange and lemonade.

Youre first in today. Its dead.

Aye? goes Scorgie sitting on a stool and looking around. The tables hadnt been cleared of the night-before-ashtrays.

Can I put some music on? asked Scorgie walking in behind the bar.

Aye help yourself.

Scorgie clattered through the big box of cassettes till he came to the yellow one. He wound it near to the end of side two then set it going. 'Reincarnated Souls' by Bunny Wailer started coming from all the speakers throughout the bar's nooks and crannies.

Thanks, says Scorgie handing over a tenner and leaving his change on the bar. He drank the drink in a one-er then asked for a lager and packet of crisps. Scorgie thought, I've twelve quid. I'll drink the lot before I leave here, then he moved round the bar to rewind the cassette again.

Scorgie moved under the blue dusk and through the nettle paths to Hacker's boathouse. He undid the wire and opened the doors pulling out the inflatable. He climbed in and took off the too-small trainers and his socks, staying sat down he reached over and opened the cock, tapped the fuel pipe and pulled the string sharp. The Yamaha rumbled smoke and a few oily water drops out the exhaust then he sunk the prop and twisted the handle on the tiller. The bow rose up and it carried him across the flat evening water. He saw dark birds hugging the surface out where the current from the loch met the sea. He took his bearing from the languid swell and mellow dipping of the lighthouse beam below the Young Crusaders Hall.

As he steered a wide curve into the bay, ruining the glassy

water beyond the buoys of his brown crab keep cages it could be seen that the conical spire of the new church in The Summer Colony also served as a lighthouse, warning the big, self-discharging vessels with their 14m drafts about the reed beds.

He cut the engine and lifted the prop as the boat cruised into shingle beach. He grit his teeth and splashed into the water and it came up to his knees. Tugging the forward cleat then the port thole he juddered the boat up the shingle and tied the nylon line to the old tree with the bark worn away to smooth wood by boat lines.

He climbed over the small sandbank. He could see the different shapes and colours of the tiles on his roof: all lifted by his own hands from a sunken barge at the end of the reed beds. From the corner he could see the lights of The Summer Colony where Sulee would be with her father, the minister, in the manse.

He would phone her after he'd showered and he would see her when he talked to them all from Pulpit Rock in the morning. He reached in the compresser door to where he hid his front door key then under the darkened sky touched by the rigid beam of light from the spire, his lips trembled words up to the stars in that holiest of hours: his return. Again, sideways through Scorgie's mind came: ... the sputter of the storm lamp held up by his brother, his father's white face where he'd lain down in The Sorrowless Rigs' burn, the empty WD40 de-seizing bottle in one hand and the sharp old baling knife in the other with both wrists split wide open but washed clean by the spate of freezing water. His dead father's face pale as Sulee's young body when she turned her back and lifted the dress that night below the Young Crusader's Hall, her ghostly arms pushing out of the summer-blue dark then the sweep of the lighthouse beam from the spire illuminating everything for just one bright instant.

(From a novel: THE FAR PLACES, 1991)

The Brown Pint of Courage

JAMES MEEK

THE SOUND OF the crickets chirping in the darkness was loud. John was aware it would upset his mum. It was years since she'd spoken but he knew what she didn't like. The noise had been going on all night. It was also overdue at the library.

John got out of bed and switched off the ghetto blaster. He took out the tape, put it in its box and put it in a pocket of his uniform jacket. He went into the kitchen.

Sorry, Mum, he shouted. Just be grateful I didn't have the tree frogs on. Did it keep you awake? I'm sorry. I'll get your breakfast. Are you wanting cereal? Aye? Are you wanting tea? Eh? If I make you tea you'll only cry it out straight away. There's never been such a woman for crying if she takes liquids. Brown tears it looks like.

John switched on the radio. The Radio Four morning discussion programme was on. A young Englishman was plugging his book. It was very difficult to make them understand, he said. But I found curiously enough that the women were much more friendly than the men. I don't mean in any sexual sense!

It's defying the laws of gravity, that's what bothers me, shouted John. If you drink it down, it should go to your stomach, not your head. The health visitor thinks I'm giving you Typhoo and milk instead of eye drops.

Yes, said Robert Robinson. But what I found interesting was the extraordinary way in which they regarded work, almost as if physical labour was the imposition of some kind of evil god.

Can you move your legs at all the day? shouted John. I'll try and be back for six. Mind and bang on the wall and someone'll maybe come if there's any trouble.

They just couldn't see the link between the coming of the rubber factory and the health care service that went with it, said the young Englishman.

John put the cereal and tea on a tray and went upstairs to his mum's room. He looked back over his shoulder as he went out.

Don't you bastards talk about me when I'm out the room, he said to Radio Four.

Once he was out the room Robert Robinson let rip a fart that was distinguishable from static even on long wave. Gammon! he said.

I'd just like to run through a few of the illustrations, said the young Englishman.

Might as well, said Robert Robinson.

John gave his mum the tea. I know you're sick, he said. I'm not so sure about this silence routine. One day I'll just pretend to go out the house and I'll really be downstairs listening and you'll be talking away, 19 to the dozen. You do that, don't you? You talk when I'm not here. Well it can't go on. I mean Christ how about a letter or something? Dear son, just to let you know I'm fine, and the tea's hardly compensation for having you. Oh no, would you stop crying? It's like living with an uncommunicative sponge. Aaaaaah! Here. Don't use your sleeve. I'll get you a jam doughnut for later. That'll be nice, eh? Don't go opening the door to any teenage conmen. And watch out for that postman – he's got his eye on you.

John put on the uniform, put a copy of *Sartor Resartus* in his trouser pocket, put on a pair of mirrored sunspecs, ran a cloth over his jet black Doc Martens, put on his helmet, climbed onto his 49cc Puch moped and rode into town. From his mum's room came music: the overture to *Showboat*.

The eyes just stared at John from under the peak of the cap, and the voice came out deep, loud.

Thick curtains of Night rushed across his soul, as rose the immeasurable Crash of Doom; and through the ruins of a shivered Universe, was he falling, falling towards the Abyss, said the Commendatore. He held the parking ticket out to John. John didn't take it. He kept his hands behind his back.

Did you write this? said the Commendatore.

No, your worship, said John. I filled in the ticket, that was my own work, it was Thomas Carlyle wrote the bit on the other side.

Did you transcribe the words of Thomas Carlyle on the ticket.

Absolutely not, your worship, said John. Absolutely no way.

The word in the canteen is that you're a man of great personal integrity and a good lad, said the Commendatore. The word on your file is you're a jumped-up piece of shite. Lying to figures in authority.

No way, your worship.

Why should anyone have written this on the ticket?

There's a blank space, Commendatore.

Spread the word. I want that space left blank. Commendatore is not right. I've got some books on Italian military ranks at home, would you like to borrow them?

No, said John.

Off you go, said the Commendatore. Tell Dek if he vomits on a private motor vehicle again he gets his cards.

Aye aye your worship, said John.

When John had gone the Commendatore went to a cupboard locked with a padlock. He took off the padlock with an individual key and took a shoebox out of the cupboard. He spread pages from the *Herald and Post* across the desk and started taking tiny pots of Humbrol enamel paint out of the box.

Can you cash a cheque? Dek asked the barman. He already had the chequebook open with a pen over the Pay line.

When the Pope comes through that door singing We Are The Fighting Billy Boys and orders a pint of special, said the barman. When. Then.

So it's yes? said Dek.

Dek! said John in the doorway.

Aye, said Dek.

It's time, said John.

Time for what, said Dek, not turning round.

Time for rightminded wardens to hit the road.

I'm not a rightminded warden. I'm a drunken warden, a bad warden, a warden wanted by sheriff officers.

Tania's worried for you, said John.

Dek lowered his head till his forehead rested on the bar. How can a man not have a few drinks if he wants? he said.

It's 8.30 in the morning, said John.

I'm not drinking early, I'm drinking late, said Dek.

The Commendatore took from the box cardboard strips. Plastic figures were glued to them, Airfix soldiers, no higher than the thumb above the joint. Their coats and peaked hats were painted black. Their faces and hands were painted pink. There were three on each strip. The Commendatore lined them up in four columns 20 deep. He bent down till his eyes were at table level and looked through their ranks for a while. He straightened up and took a slender-tipped brush from the box. He sucked it to a fine point and dipped it in a pot of yellow enamel. He picked up three plastic figures and brought them up close to his face. The tip of the brush approached the first figure's head and the Commendatore started to paint a yellow band round its hat.

Have you ever done a Rolls? said Tania.

Rollers don't park, said Dek. They grace the street. There's an old Edinburgh bylaw says Rolls Royce owners may requisition traffic wardens to lick the salt off their bodywork during inclement weather. He stopped and leaned against a wall with his eyes closed.

Are you OK? said Tania.

I think I left something in the pub, said Dek.

Your wages, said John.

If you could feel what I feel you wouldn't be funny about it, said Dek. Wait. I'm out of balance. The right side of my body's got more than the left side.

John went up to him and looked him over. Try lifting your right leg, he said.

Dek lifted his right leg. John hooked his boot under Dek's left ankle and pulled. Dek fell over.

Is that better? said John.

Bastard! said Dek, trying to clutch at John. He got up and started limping after him.

Keep going, you'll even it up, said John, disappearing round the corner. Dek stopped and bent double, his hands on his knees, coughing.

Are you OK? said Tania.

Dek puked on the pavement. Aye, fine, he said, straightening up.

Do you want a mint? said Tania, holding out a packet of Polos.

Dek looked at the Polos. He looked at Tania's face. Do you use these? he said, frowning.

No, she said, I don't like them. They might help settle your stomach.

Aye, said Dek, taking a Polo. Thanks. You should try them.

Outside the games shop a driver opened the back of a delivery truck. He looked round. A traffic warden was watching him.

Won't be a moment, said the driver.

You can't park here, said Tania.

I'm must making a delivery.

I'll walk round the block, said Tania. You'd better be finished. She walked away. The driver climbed into the back of the truck. There was another traffic warden.

What? said the driver.

You can't park here, said Dek.

Your friend said it was all right for a minute, said the driver.

Dek looked at his watch. I'm starting the clock, he said. You've got sixty seconds. He strolled off with his hands behind his back, singing 'Only 24 Hours from Tulsa'.

The driver pushed a box to the tailgate and jumped down. Jesus Christ, he said.

You can't park here, said John.

I'm searching for the hidden camera, said the driver.

There's a yellow line, sir, said John.

There's just one of you, isn't there, and you're going round and round, said the driver.

Tania appeared next to John. You still here? she said, taking out her ticket pad.

Next time I'll take the bus, said the driver.

Dek came strolling back. That's your minute up, he said.

So, said the driver. What do you want?

What've you got? said John.

Scruples, said the driver, handing him a box.

The Commendatore picked up another rank of figures. One of the figures had a skirt. He painted yellow bands on the figures' hats and set the group apart from the rest. He put his brush in a jar of turps and rested his chin on his hands, looked at the separate group of three.

One potato, two potato, three potato, four. She loves me not, he said.

John's mum sat in her chair, gripping the wooden armrests. The record was stuck in a groove in Ol' Man River. Sick of tryin', it played, sick of tryin', sick of tryin'. John's mum looked for an hour at the piece of wallpaper that was peeling off at the right hand side of the mantelpiece. Suddenly, without warning, she began looking at the cracked tile on the fireplace.

John devoured a black pudding roll. He picked a card.

Come on then, said Dek, shaking the dice.

Mouth full, said John, reading the card to himself.

Come on!

I'm not sure about this one.

Come on, said Tania, we've already had the one about skiving.

We're not skiving, said John, we're in a meeting.

For God's sake, said Dek. He snatched the card off John and read it out. One of your best friends has got very bad breath. Would you tell them?

Tricky, said John.

No, it's easy, said Tania. Of course you'd tell them. No bother. Folk've got to be told so's they can sort themselves out.

Dek? said John.

Oh . . . I don't know really. Aye, I suppose, I'd tell them.

I wouldn't, said John. And neither would you, absolutely no way.

I would! said Dek.

We'll settle this outside, said John. Tania, do us a favour and stay here.

OK, said Tania. Once Dek and John were outside the cafe she started reading the cards that hadn't been turned up yet.

Outside John said to Dek: You are a liar.

Look, I'll tell her sometime, OK, said Dek.

Every time she opens her mouth it's like a hot day in the elephant house, and you sit there and let her think she's fine!

She's not that bad.

Not that bad? It smells like something's died in there. The nearest thing she's ever had to a toothbrush in her mouth is the dry bits from a caramel wafer.

You tell her then, said Dek.

You're the one who fancies her, said John.

Oh, Christ, said Dek. If it wasn't for the halitosis she'd

be my dream woman. What if I put Listerine in her Bacardi instead of lemonade.

Just do like you said and tell her, said John. Buy her a selection box of toothpaste and a fancy brush.

I don't know, said Dek.

How can she turn you down? said John. You're a single man with a steady job, a nice council flat, a drink problem and £5,000 worth of debt. She's bound to go for you. Women like a man with big ideas about credit.

A Fiat Panda was parking on double yellow lines. Tania and Dek watched with their arms folded while it approached the kerb, approached, reversed, inched back, inched forward, mounted the pavement and stopped. The driver got out and walked off down the road with a couple of empty carrier bags. Tania and Dek stopped him with a hand on each shoulder.

Red sky in the morning, shepherd's warning, said Dek.

Yellow lines in the street, driver he will greet, said Tania.

The man shook his head and smiled. He walked over to the car and tapped the windscreen. Disabled sticker, he said.

Oh right, said Dek. What's wrong with you?

Nothing. It's my wife, she's disabled. She's at home.

So you're not disabled?

No. But I've got the sticker. There's no problem, is there?

Normally there would be, said Dek. But we're able to bend the rules to help people. He put his hand on the man's shoulder, drew back his foot and booted him on the right knee. The man collapsed, screaming.

That's OK now, sir, said Dek.

John marched alone down Leith Walk, booking all the blue

cars. He took his break at noon. He went to a library and changed his crickets tape for one called *Sounds of the Great Rift Valley*. He bought his mum's doughnut and a cold bridie. He sat down on a bench and took out his book.

A car parked on the double yellow line a few yards away. A woman got out with a measuring tape, some chalk and a camera. She made measurements and drew crosses on the pavement.

John ate his bridie and watched. The woman took pictures of the crosses.

Is this street theatre? said John.

No, said the woman.

I like the fire eaters and the jugglers, and the ones that pretend balloons are heavy.

Should you not be away wheelclamping invalid cars or something? said the woman.

I'm on my break, said John. Piece in our time. Do you want a bit of my bridie?

No.

It's very tasty. Or I could read to you: It is the Night of the World, and still long till it be Day: we wander amid the glimmer of smoking ruins, and the Sun and the Stars of Heaven are as blotted out for a season.

That's Thomas Carlyle, said the woman.

John shouted Yes! and stood up.

I'm from the council, said the woman, coming over.

So am I!

I'm Gillian, from monuments. We're taking pictures of this place before they cover it with the community drama and merchant banking complex.

You should put up a plaque to the unknown warden. That's me, John, the unknown warden.

Gillian stepped back, put her feet together and described an area of the pavement with her hands. It was here, she said, that Carlyle saved himself from despair. He'd become a man with an emptiness where his spirit used to be. He'd lost faith in God, and belief in the Devil. He'd lost faith in love. He saw no rewards in heaven or punishments in hell. His sense of right and wrong seemed like rubbish left behind by illusions of God. It seemed that people just lived afraid of pain, and wanting pleasure. He could imagine people finding a reason for living in their work, but he had no work to show for his time on earth. He was 28 years old. Something inside him was angry but it didn't seem to have anything to do with the boredom of the universe he was stuck in. He hardly noticed other people, they were like parts in a machine to him. The world was the machine, and it didn't do him the favour of wanting him to suffer. No, because it ground him down automatically. He would have killed himself, but there was a small bit of religious teaching stuck in his brain, and anyway, he couldn't be bothered. And all the while he felt frightened. He didn't know what he was afraid of. Until he came here, to Leith Walk, and one moment he didn't know and the next moment he knew. He was frightened of death, nothing more or less, because in the end that was all there was to be afraid of. And when he knew it, he looked at death, and he said: Come on, then. I'll meet you and I'll take you on. He stood here, a man still young, miserable with the grey world and his being lost in it, and he reached out over forty years ahead and shouted at death that he could see it hiding there and it might as well come out because he could look at it and still live on as a free man until the final reckoning came. And he felt so strong and angry after that, burning up with hatred for death, and so he was alive.

John was quiet for a bit. Then he said: Let's call our first child Leith.

My surname's Walker.

Well, mine's Keith.

Come on, finish your bridie and go back to work.

John got up and stood closer to Gillian. Your hair's just like the adverts, he said. It smells like turkish delight.

Tania was in the Commendatore's office. He'd put up a folding screen in one corner.

I'm supposed to be meeting someone, she said.

This won't take long, said the Commandatore. I've designed a new uniform for the wardens. I'd like you to try it on. It's behind that screen. Just to give you extra reassurance I'll put this blindfold on while you're changing.

Do I get some kind of bonus for this? said Tania.

Probably, said the Commendatore, tying on the blindfold. I can't see a thing now. This is made out of one of my old uniforms. Have you found it all right? Are you getting changed?

Yeah, said Tania.

You know, Thomas Carlyle would've liked your legs and your ankle boots, said John. He would've loved your red suit. He wouldn't have been able to stop himself sighing when he thought how good it would be to place his hands on your waist and kiss your neck.

Aah! said the Commendatore, taking off the blindfold. It looks wonderful. Here, look in the mirror.

Oh, said Tania.

What do you think?

You know those dreams you have? When you forget to put any clothes on and you go to work and you fall into a bath of golden syrup and when you get out people are throwing little strips of Argos catalogue at you and they stick to your body and everybody starts pointing at you and shouting Breakfast! Breakfast! I think it's worse than that.

The trouble is you just don't understand it. Look. These tassels at the back of the cap conceal a zip. I open the zip, put in my hand, and hey presto – a green eyeshade which fits onto the peak of the cap for bright sunshine. No more unsightly sunglasses.

He would've loved to look into your eyes, said John, removing his sunglasses and putting them in his pocket. He looked into Gillian's eyes. She blinked. He would've loved to feel your lips against his own.

They kissed.

Your time's up! shouted John, running over to her car and pulling out his ticket pad.

You complete bastard! yelled Gillian.

Rules are rules, said John, scribbling as fast as he could.

Don't think you won't suffer for this, said Gillian. She made a run at him and pulled his hat off.

Tss, said John. He stuck the parking ticket under the wiper.

Jane Carlyle would've loved to see this hat go, said Gillian, taking out a lighter and setting fire to the cap. It flared up and she dropped it on the pavement.

See that? said John. No health and safey measures at all. What if I'd been struck by lightning? I'd be dead meat.

You are dead meat.

I'm going now, said John, and walked away.

The shoulder-tabs are based on a Soviet design, said the Commendatore. They're not practical, but they help give the uniform a more imposing look. Then you've got your waistbelt, with water-bottle, smog mask, quick release ticket pad holder, A to Z and spare shoelaces.

It feels hot and heavy, said Tania.

Does it? said the Commendatore. Here, sit down. Do you want a drink? I've got some rum.

Thanks, said Tania.

Dek looked at the clock behind the bar. It said 1.15. He drank down the half pint that was left in his glass in a oner and ordered another, with a whisky chaser.

Terrible to be stood up, he said.

What time were you supposed to meet her? said the barman.

Five past. Tell you what, make it a double. I've given her ten whole minutes. Well into the excess period.

No waiting on weekdays except for loading or unloading, said the barman.

Dek pointed the finger at him. Right, he said. Listen. Leave the warden jokes to the wardens. That's my lass we're talking about. He took the fresh pint of heavy and three-quarters drained it.

Tania sipped rum. She sat with her legs crossed in the Commendatore's chair, brushing pretend fluff off the ski pants-style black trousers with yellow piping he had designed. The Commendatore sat on the edge of the desk with his arms folded, looking down at her. He reached out a hand and began fiddling with one of her shoulder tabs. Tania cleared her throat and looked in the opposite direction.

You're the most beautiful of the traffic wardens under my command, said the Commendatore. Call me romantic if you like, call me oldfashioned, but when I see you sitting there so sweet and lovely, only one thing comes into my mind: Sex.

Tania coughed.

Let's do it now, said the Commendatore, standing up and taking hold of both her shoulders. Let's take off our clothes here and now and have sex. Come on.

No, said Tania.

Why not? said the Commendatore. He found a tiny pocket on one of her sleeves, opened a Velcro tab and pulled out a packet. Look! he said. The traffic warden of tomorrow will be Aids-conscious and free from unwanted pregnancies.

No, said Tania, getting up and going over to the door. I don't want to have sex with you.

Why not?

Because you're thirty years older than me, I don't like you and you're very, very ugly.

The clock behind the bar said 1.30. Dek was drinking them as fast as the barman could pull them. He had beer on his shoes, on his trousers, on his jacket, on his hair, up his nose and on the small of his back. Tania came into the bar.

My God, said the barman. It's the provisional wing of the Salvation Army.

Dek swivelled on his stool and blinked at Tania through the beer in his eyes. He raised his arm and pointed it at her as best he could, swinging it about 45 degrees in all directions. Your time's up! he shouted. No feeding the meter. He fell off the stool and writhed at the bottom of it. Tania went over and hauled him to his feet.

How did he get like this? said Tania to the barman. I was only twenty-five minutes late.

Thirsty.

Did you have to help him with it so much?

Just taking orders.

Get us a taxi, then.

From his window on the third floor the Commendatore watched Tania helping Dek into a taxi. She was having problems with the special belt he had designed. Dek had got somehow caught up in it. They struggled for a while at the edge of the pavement, Dek tugging at his coat, Tania trying to push him into the cab. After a while the driver got out to help. In the end Tania unfastened the belt and dropped it in the road. They got into the taxi and drove off.

The Commendatore went to the cupboard where he kept the model wardens. He took out the strip of three with one figure with a skirt. With a pair of nail scissors he snipped the strip in three. He picked up the two male figures in turn and cut off their heads and their legs, then put them in his mouth and chewed them. Still chewing, he laid the female figure down in an ashtray, lit a match and set fire to it. The painted plastic burned well. In a few seconds it was a sizzling yellow maggot. Soon after that it was a black stain on the ashtray. The Commendatore spat the chewed-up figures into the ashtray. He left the office and went home.

John got home just before six. He went to see his mum. Sick of tryin', sick of tryin', sick of tryin', said the record player. John lifted the record off the turntable and put it in its sleeve.

You see, I know you can move, he said. This record is on every day when I come back. How come you always put on the one with the scratch, instead of the new one I got? Here's your doughnut. Yes, you can eat well enough, can't you. I don't have to be Sherlock Holmes to see you've been getting up to go to the toilet. And that's a good thing, I'm not saying it's not. But just supposing you left that chair once when I was actually here, in the house, me, myself, your son. I met a girl today. The same sex as you in fact, except she chooses to walk and talk. If we had a phone I'd probably call her tonight, if I had her number. My name's on the ticket I gave her. She could find the number of my work and get in touch. We could go out if you got better. No need, anyway, she could just come round, and she could talk to you like I'm doing now, talk and talk and talk and talk and talk, and it wouldn't make any difference, because you never say anything or do anything, you just sit there. And cry sometimes. Oh, not now, not this time. Don't cry again. How can your face get so wet so quickly? I'll get your tea.

John wiped his mum's face and went and cooked fish fingers under the grill. He served them with tomato sauce and peas and mashed potato. He cut up the fish fingers on his mum's plate and put them on a tray with a mug of juice and his mum's prescribed drugs. He took the food up to her and ate it with her while they watched *Reporting Scotland* and *Channel Four News*. He left the TV on and went down to do the washing up. He went to his room and put the *Great Rift Valley* tape on. He looked at the cover notes. Baboons to kick off with. John fell asleep.

Outside the games shop a driver unrolled the back of a delivery truck. Traffic wardens arrived.

Remember us? said John.

Yes. The driver took a box out of the truck. Go, he said.

Go?

Go!

OK, OK, keep your shirt on, said Dek, taking the box.

Go, read John from the instruction book, is an ancient Chinese game of pure mental skill. Its rules are simpler than chess but the tactics are so much more complicated that as yet no computer has been programmed to play successfully. To succeed at Go requires an agile mind, a clear head and a patient soul. There is no clear ending to a game of Go. Play ends when both players agree they have nothing to gain by continuing.

Let's see that, said Dek, taking the book from John. He wiped his hands free of bacon fat with a napkin, made the book lie open flat with his fist and put on a pair of reading glasses. Tania took the board out of the box. It was a hinged block of wood with a plain grid marked on it. She moved the salt cellar and brown sauce bottle to make room for it on the table and opened it out. The only other things in the box were the counters: porcelain discs, one set matt black, the other set glazed white.

Dek looked up from the book and picked a black disc. Stones, he said, looking at it over the top of his glasses and turning it in his fingers. They call them stones. I think I can handle this.

John was drying his mum's hair with a towel. Christ, Mum, you're going bald, he said. He rubbed like he was sanding a plank. He bent down and looked in her face. Only joking, he said. Wee grin? No, OK.

Someone chapped at the front door. John went to see. It was Tania, still in uniform.

Seen Dek? she said. He wasn't in the pub.

Last time I saw him he was heading off with that game in his bag, said John. Thought he might be trying to swap it for a drink. Frankie Boy's chessboard's starting to get a bit worn.

No, he wasn't there. I think we should go over and see if he's all right.

Aye, us and the rest of the Broons, said John. I can't come out, I'm doing my mum's hair.

I'll give you a hand, then, said Tania. They went upstairs. John's mum's hair was dry, combed and lashed in a tight bun.

Some excuse, said Tania.

See you? said John, shaking his finger at his mum. You've got a lot to answer for. Can you not run away and join a circus or something? I'm away out. Listen, when I come back I want this place looking like a new pin.

John only had the one crash helmet for his moped. It took Tania and him an hour and a half to get to Dek's place what with the evening buses and the walking.

He's got a special knock so's he knows we're not the men from Barclaycard, said John, it's some Dusty Springfield number, I can't mind which. Could be 'You Don't Have to Say You Love Me'.

Dek! shouted Tania through the letterbox. It's Tania and John!

They heard his footsteps in the hall and he opened the door.

What's wrong? he said.

It's nine o'clock and you're sober, said John.

They went straight through to the lounge. It was kind of bare but neat, just a bit of dust on Dek's maritime books and his models of tea clippers, and the usual unrinsed glasses were missing. Dek had the Go board laid out on the coffee table, which was pushed up close to the armchair with the deepest bum-hollow. A game was in progress, the black and white discs all mingled up with each other on the board in a complex pattern. John and Tania sat down on the settee together. Dek went back to the armchair and studied the board, rubbing his chin.

How about a coffee when you're done playing with yourself, said John.

I can't do it, said Dek.

Well, tea'd be fine. Or a can of something, if you've got it. Maybe a light salad, something inventive with chick peas and a twist of lemon, wee soupçon of garlic in there.

I can't do it. These stones . . . white does this, black does this, then white does the same thing, there's no end to it. I've been trying to crack it for two hours.

Tania and John went over and knelt on the carpet by the table. It seemed Dek had got into a situation where the black and white pieces were stalemated on one corner of the board. Black could take a white piece, but then white could immediately take the black piece that did the taking, and then white could take the black piece that took the white piece – there was no way out.

I can't stand looking at this, said John. These black circles, I feel like God cruising over all the wardens on parade. I'll make the coffee. He went to the kitchen.

Where's the instruction book? said Tania.

Ach, I've read it backwards, said Dek, staring at the board and biting his nails.

Where is it?

Dek nodded to his right. Tania picked up the book. After a while she said Ko.

Eh? said Dek.

Ko, said Tania. It says here if black and white reach a position of ko, where a cycle of capture and counter-capture can continue indefinitely, the player whose piece is captured first has to make a move elsewhere on the board.

Where'd you find that? said Dek, grabbing the book.

Two of the pages were stuck together, said Tania.

Dek lifted the pages to his nostrils. Bacon fat, he said. Ko. OK.

OK, said Tania. You did say you'd read it backwards,.

Dek looked in Tania's eyes. I, eh . . . wait a minute, don't go away, he said, and went off to the kitchen.

Who's winning, the wardens or those white creatures? said John.

Dek opened the fridge and took out a can.

We're all winning, everyone except me, he said. He took a pint glass out of a cupboard and pulled the can open. She's perfect for me, I just can't say anything.

You need a drink, said John.

Right, said Dek.

John took the can from Dek and poured the contents brown and foaming down the plughole.

You arse. Ninety-nine pence, said Dek.

Now for the drink, said John. He held the empty can up in front of Dek. What does it say?

Best English bitter, said Dek.

The big letters.

Courage.

Right. John lifted the pint glass, tilted it slightly and rested the edge of the can carefully on the rim. You have to watch this, he said. If you get the angle wrong it foams up like spit in a sherbet fountain. Are you thirsty?

Yeah, I was kind of, aye.

Cause this is the best thing out for thirst. D'you remember telling me about your first love, Elaine Corkwood?

Course I do.

D'you remember that time you were going to ask her out?

I suppose.

How did you feel? Hot and sweaty?

Uhuh.

And your whole chest was shaking with your heart going, your mouth was really dry, your tongue felt like a cold smoked sausage, you kept dry-swallowing and trying to lick your lips. It was like that, wasn't it?

Yeah.

So what did you do? Sounds like you were thirsty, did you go down to the pub?

I was twelve years old!

Right. You didn't go to the pub. You had some of this stuff. Under-age drinking, the best. You knocked back some of the courage and you went ahead and asked her out.

Yeah, and she told me to fuck off.

Whoah! Just a moment. The pouring is about to begin. John gradually tilted the empty can. Its colour is golden-brown, he said, it's cool and translucent, with a taste between malt and honey, and a mountain burn. Look at the way it curls when it hits the glass, there's a freshness about it. Just watching that stream makes me feel better. There we go. D'you mind if I have a wee sip? John put the glass to his lips, tilted it slightly, took it away from his mouth, closed his eyes, smiled and shivered. He opened his eyes and handed the glass to Dek.

Dek took it and looked at it.

Go on, said John.

Dek lifted the glass to his mouth, rested the rim on his teeth and jerked it upwards.

Steady! said John. You'll spill it. Take it in one, but take it steady. Christ, you've had enough practice.

Dek began to tilt the glass at a measured pace, eyes closed, thrapple working.

Good! said John.

The glass went up to and over the horizontal. Dek put it down, wiped his mouth with the back of his hand and broke wind.

OK? said John.

Ko, said Dek, and headed for the lounge.

Eh . . . ko, said John. He opened his mouth wide, held his head back and shook the glass upside down over it.

Dek faced Tania in the lounge. Listen, he said, I think we should maybe try going out, you and me.

Och Dek.

There's something I'd like you to do for me, though.

John and Dek left the dental hospital after midnight. John paid for a cab back to Dek's. In the taxi Dek took out a white porcelain piece from the Go set.

I suppose it does look a wee bit like a mint, he said. How did she have to bite it so hard?

It shows she was passionate about you. It's the best thing that could've happened, said John. They'll sort her out in there. I don't think she's been to a dentist since she left school.

Right enough, see the gleam in that guy's eye when they wheeled her in.

Big special in the dental magazines, eh.

Aye. Full dental centre spread. Whoaugh.

Steady man.

When Dek and John entered the Commendatore's office he hurled traffic safety pamphlets at them.

I've always wanted to do that, he said. Throw the book at you. He leaned back in his chair and folded his hands on his stomach.

They're not books, they're pamphlets, and politically suspect as well, said John. Look. See how the cars only drive on one side of the road? The *left* side of the road? See? Get my drift? That Department of Transport's nothing but a nest of communists, if you ask me.

I didn't, did I? said the Commendatore. That's your problem. You're a smartarse. Nobody loves a smartarse. You're out. God knows the punters hate us enough already without you inflicting mysterious extracts from Victorian literature on them. And there's no place in my department for wardens who discriminate against cars on the basis of colour. You can clear your locker now.

He turned to Dek. As for you, apart from your body's not very special ability to turn beer into piss and vomit, you've assaulted a disabled driver.

Ach, come on, he wasn't disabled until I kicked him.

Oh! Two for the price of one, thank you, said the Commendatore, making a note.

Christ, said Dek in wonderment, I've been out of school for 25 years, and you still sound like my teacher.

John sat down on the edge of the pavement outside the wardens' office. He looked over at his moped. Someone had stuck a ticket on it. He lowered his head, took out his P45 and started folding it into a paper aeroplane, with his shoulders hunched and his arms hanging between his knees.

Dek came out, sat down beside him and spat in the gutter.

Shite, he said.

John said nothing.

Charlie's fixed up a meeting with the branch secretary, Dek said.

John said nothing.

Industrial action or a tribunal at least, Dek said. He turned to John and shouted. Hello! Hello . . . Hello!

John launched the P45 aircraft. It went a few yards and nosedived into the road. The Grand Inquisitor was right, he said, nobody loves a smartarse.

Ach, stop feeling sorry for yourself. Dek took out a big hipflask, unscrewed the top and offered it to John. John took it, shook it, sniffed it, turned it upside down and gave it back.

It's empty, he said.

I filled it before I left. It's courage, said Dek, putting the flask to his lips and throwing his head back. John watched as he gulped it down.

Hey, he said. Leave some for us, eh. He took the flask and swigged. It's not so good warm, he said.

What's Tania going to say? said Dek. Bankrupt and unemployed.

What's my mother going to say. Fuck all. She's like her song. She must know somethin, but she don't say nothin. Thomas Carlyle could've written Ol' Man River. He probably did. You can see him in his top hat and tails, tramping down Leith Walk with his face done up like Al Jolson, jumping up on a conveniently placed bale of cotton and singing I gets weary, and sick of tryin, I'm tired of livin, and scared of dyin.

Aaah, that's good stuff, said Dek, finishing the courage. Fuck the tribunal. Come on. Let's go and play with the traffic.

They struck just before the evening rush hour, and no-one realised what was happening at first. Dek concentrated on the city centre while John used his moped to hit key points further out. Their main tactic was to direct streams of cars back on each other, creating self-perpetuating tailbacks in both directions. By seven o'clock the Forth Bridge, the A1, the A8 and the bypass were all locked solid. At an early stage the traffic police asked the wardens to help them out, causing added confusion when it was realised who was responsible. A number of wardens were arrested. Others were attacked by angry motorists who had heard radio reports about an army of rogue wardens who, according to a spokesman for the Automobile Association, deserved to be shot on sight. Thousands of vehicles ran out of petrol while idling in the queues and drivers bedded down in their cars. Next day the papers gave prominence to the woman who had given birth in her car overnight and planned to call her daughter Montego.

Dek and John got six months each. The sheriff loved his vintage Bentley and wanted to give them more but the charges were too obscure. The accused were seen to drink from imaginary glasses before sentence was passed. In jail Dek perfected the art of Go and began to correspond with the Japanese masters. Tania was the subject of a long article in the *British Dental Journal*, explaining why it had been necessary to remove all her teeth. When Dek got out the two of them moved into a hard-to-let in the schemes, where they occasionally hosted frightened visitors from Kyoto and Osaka. The Commendatore retired shortly after the great snarl-up, rewarded for his long and selfless service with an OBE and haemorrhoids.

Dek and John's deeds caused a rethink on traffic flow in Leith Walk and the community drama and merchant banking complex was cancelled. After his release John called Gillian and explained this had been his intention all along. Gillian wasn't as grateful as he'd hoped because she'd started sleeping with one of the merchant bankers and was enjoying it. But they could be friends.

John ground his teeth and asked her out to the pictures. Afterwards they headed back to his place. He spent the journey explaining his mother.

She'll sit there and look at you and cry, he said. She'll do nothing, say nothing. It's terrible.

Back at the house John made Gillian wait in the hall while he went upstairs to his mum's room. She wasn't there. They found her in the kitchen, with the table all laid out for three, with a white cloth, tea and a jam sponge. John put his hands on his hips and shook his head.

You are a truly terrible woman, he said.

His mother and Gillian looked at him. Gillian laughed. John's mother started to cry. John and Gillian sat down and the three of them began to eat the cake.

Submission

PAUL REEKIE

YOU WOULDN'T RECOGNISE the milieu, the set up, you'd find me in nowadays Davie. These young guys. They have a basketball in the living room, but they don't play basketball. It's skateboards and folders and folders of their spray-paint art. Deedee asked me if I wanted a mural in my bedroom. Told him I don't want a bedroom like an underpass. Was he going to like pish in the corner to make it authentic. Johnny B— who's the same age as me; when he's telling his girlfriend he's going to watch football on the TV says, 'I'm going to watch *the ball game.*' You get a laugh. It's good. Don't mind their records; two decks and 16 track going most the time. I can't watch TV anymore; I'm not physically able. I found that when I saw adverts or anything that unexpectedly turned me on, gave me a hard-on, I was in a lot of pain. I'll have to tell you about my warning shot from the Gods.

Mary (a painter) put turpentine down the toilet and I dropped a fag into it while I sat doing my meditations. I'm sitting with a nappy on as I write this. Arse, baws, knob all burnt. I go to the Infirmary and they put this spray on it. What have they given me for a pain-killer? Nurofen. It's fucking useless. The skin splits if I get a hard-on or am not *very* careful in the bog. You remember that old John The Postman record 'Tooth ache'? A fine representation of intense pain; well it's worse than that. Much worse.

Thanks for the MS Davie. I'll check with it seeing as I have the leisure. You ask about some of the Old Gang, the Old Faces; to tell you'll be quite hard. You ask me to spare you nothing. I've no chance of remembering the lot. You ask how to get in the writing game and where to send stuff. I'll send you the address of Jock's magazine. But Davie you are a young cat yet, if you want a novel out, just sleep with those Bloomsbury women and you get any old stuff out. Look at Graham Barrie. It's tiresome you know, sending out the old brown envelope on spec.

Mind you, novels are all shite to me. The novelist on Mt Olympus shunting his poor characters about. Novels are full of padding – they're clearly objectionable. Maybe I shouldn't've read Proust though or all those English novels, that, frivolous or in earnest were big on family values. How To Write That Novel: Get a prose style together. Don't worry if you have a story or not but you MUST have that System Of Symbols together. Even the nowadays tape-recorder novel is shite. Somebody's got to outline the vernacular and that. Aye. But what a fucking chore. 'I am a tape recorder' is no more true today than 'I am a camera' was true in the 1930's. Listening to the guys in the house the other day, I was reminded of when Jock did a big reading at the Tramway in Glasgow. He was back-stage after his set and this rock group were muttering amongst themselves, 'Scottish people shouldn't say, "motherfucker". Man, Scottish people can say any motherfucking thing they like. These are all very *fleeting* thoughts though Davie. Seems as if nobody's allowed not to be a philosopher, or not to be a polemicist. That'll be the end for poetry then; not a bad thing necessarily? The charity shops will be stocked with even more tweeds, more corduroy trousers, yea even unto the broon brogues.

The Old Gang, The Old Faces: One I heard about the other day was Boogie, Diane's big brother. He was adopted. Adopted by a good family though. He thought it was a shame for himself. Made sure you knew it was a shame for him. I remember he had all those WW2 magazines in the binders. I mean this is at 16. Airfix kits, Commando Comics. Even that Lockhead And The Starfighters LP, the solo one by the guy in Hawkwind. He wore all that army navy store gear. Boogie loved all of that military hardwear. Maybe it's not a big deal. Like in our fathers' day it was choo-choo trains. Compared to when Boogie and I were at school, kids seem to love rockets less and monsters more. What I heard was he works, writes for *Jane's Defence Monthly*. That'll suit him. I've still got his mother's *Complete Shakespeare*, her name inside and everything. Maybe he doesn't want it back because it's not his real mum. It's amazing how timid, how reactionary a person can be when they think they're unloved.

Communist George, he's another one. I still see him. He gave me this 1970's pamphlet 'Homage to John McLean'. Some of the good old jock poets in that. Edwin Morgan the best of the bunch therein. George is running icons out of the Ukraine nowadays. And it is a lucrative trade. He brought back this first-day cover from the Ukraine with this stamp of it, 'Derek Dick(Fish) Scottish poet and writer' with his noble head sideways-on like the Queen. And this is what passes for jock poets over there. Remember we went to see Yevtushenko reading at the King's Theatre. That poem about the silver birch, when he was crouched up in a ball on the stage, slowly growing like a tree as the poem went. Like you did at nursery school. Effective though, else I'd've forgotten it. Christ, we saw Nureyev dance in the Ballet Russe the same year. *L'Après-midi d'un faune* and all the American tourists around us saying, 'He sure can't jump as high anymore . . . He's getting old.' I bet none of them knew at that time he was a hiver.

George though, what is he like? He's in amongst all these 19 yr old Ukrainians. He says where else can an old cat like him get off with all these young girls. They're always wanting to bring the whole family to the west. George is forever asking me if I know any jobs for artists. I have to tell him like it's not my line, George. Go and see Demarco or that. But I think the time the family are becoming in evidence is about the time when George takes his icons and splits.

Davie I'll tell you the biggest laugh. No I'll tell you later.

She reached down into her knickers, pulled out a bloodied Lil-let and threw it at the band. I can't remember which band. Maybe The Flowers. I don't want to go on about punk bands and all that Davie. I know you're into it but I find that there's a lot of the enthusiasms of my youth that I just can't get a hard-on for anymore (like if I could get one at all). So she threw the fanny-pad and I thought – that's the girl for me. We got off. We met at gigs and wrote to each other.

When Kelly was 17 she went to St Gerard's in Govan, the same school Billy Connolly went to. She sent me some poems:

> *Stuff my cunt with broken glass*
> *Stick your cock right up my arse*

Precocious work. Kelly's parents had a book *Kiss of the Whip*, a pseudo-scientific book on flogging, like on the bookshelf in the living room. The family bible.

Another of Kelly's verses treated of her first sexual experiences: stripping off in the dark, in the cupboard under the stairs; skelping her bare arse with a ruler. She had no English blood either, only Scottish-Irish. I gave her that Angela Carter book *The Sadeian Woman* and she fairly lapped that up. There was a carfuffle about this punk group called The Moors Murderers so we had to read Emlyn William's book on Brady and Hindley. Now Ian Brady had a secret library that he had hidden in a suitcase in a locker. *Kiss of the Whip* was one of the books he had. Kelly wanted her own secret library stacked up in the bedroom. I agreed to help. She called it the Kentral library.

In no time at all the paraphernalia she wanted began to accrue around her: plastic belts in gaudy colours, a frayed piece of rope, a wig, hardly the full accoutrement of the dungeon. But, the books. It's hard to get into all that claustrophobic S&M nowadays, but you had to go to extraordinary lengths to get books. A lot of Sade wasn't published in Britain in the late 70's so it was sending away to New York for Sade in English (international money orders and commission to pay to a broker for finding out what the exchange rate is). I remember having that cartoon *Story of O* and *120 Days of Sodom* seized by HM customs. Did you ever get one of those letters? 'Such goods are obscene . . . legalese . . . bullshit . . . will take action to condemn thereof.'

I remember in one letter she told me about when she'd been in her bedroom putting the heavy eye make-up on, dressing up as a punk to go out. Her father came in and smashed the hand mirror off the wall. Her father had been an accountant at a ship yard but hadn't worked for 12 years because of a bad leg. Kelly became wistful when she told of the days when she and her sisters all had good winter coats. *Such beautiful little coats.*

Her mother worked for the Labour Party, and also had a

secretarial job at the RAC. She was called Kelly as well –
don't laugh Davie – I mean they shared the same first names.
She told me that her mother made it with the boss at the RAC
job. I wish I'd known before I phoned up one day and got her
father on the phone, 'Kelly? Kelly? Which Kelly is it you're
wanting? There's *two* Kelly's live here. Which Kelly, eh, which
Kelly?' On and on like this. He had the Irish side in him, and
she painted him to me as the classic tyrant along the lines of
Eugene O'Neill, etc. She told me she had to get away from
Glasgow; from her father, from having to sell her mother's
medicine cabinet up the Mars Bar to get records, from the
rows: that's why she was at university.

She lived on Fettes Row and I was living in Bernard St.
She wrote me all the time. This was when she studied
English literature and classics. Rows of the black-spined
Penguin classics by the bed. That was when Thucydides
was 'Sook The Diddies'. A desk in the lecture hall had *first
year girls suck cock* on it and she wrote next to it *yum yum*.
William Wordsworth's birthplace was Cockermouth . . . you
can imagine. She copied me out passages of *The Prelude*. I don't
have them now. What could they have been? I can hardly look
at the book, but I know the passages didn't include: *The poet,
gentle creature as he is/Has like the lover his unruly times – his
fits when he is neither sick nor well/Though no distress be near
him but his own unmanageable thoughts.*

Davie imagine my perturbation, in fact I was right pissed
off at what that lassie said in the paper. She came to meet us
in the pub at 11 o'clock on a Friday night. I said to her firstly
that we get enough creepy journos hanging around us. They
want Edinburgh gossip – they can fuck off. I'm sure that's
why we got slagged for our drinking, smoking, raving. The
evidence of her own eyes, but Friday night 11–3 (her early

bedtime) there's plenty going on. No, I don't mind having the tale told on us for that; that we are disorganised, are wasters, or having described the common or garden procrastination that anyone would recognise. Aye. Fine. No Davie. What was very irritating was to be described as *incomprehensible*. Put me in mind of this academic-type I met recently who asked, 'What are you doing nowadays?' I said I was looking at some Tudor bawdry.

'That'll sound great with your accent.'

Christopher and Brian mind, were going to be film directors. They were at university but really wanted to be at film school. It was movies, movies, movies with them all the time. Someone built a joint in front of them, it was oh I don't like those Cheech and Chong films. If they're sitting with a couple of girls you'll overhear, 'I don't think *The Maltese Falcon* is misogynistic' and so on. They ran the film club though and we could go and see films anytime for nowt. We saw them all. I remember this Japanese film, *Diary of a Shinjuku Thief* I think it was called. It starts in black and white. Guy goes in the bookshop and pinches Genet's *Thief's Journal* (heavy irony). There's some business about a romance but this isn't clear. The young hero gets caught pinching a book. It swings into 16mm colour footage of the Tokyo riots at the end; good punk stuff but Brian said it was 'very 60's'.

Christopher and Brian moved next door to us at 13 Bernard St. Hippies lived there. They had a wooden plaque on the front door with a toadstool painted on it. A hippie guy that lived there fancied Kelly so I had her borrow his complete bound editions of *Evergreen Review*. Most of the stories and poems in them you could find in other books, but the adverts were the best. There was one from about 1959; it had a cartoon of a guy in black beard and tights holding a book, while a sexy girl is swooning at his feet. The copy goes: Things you need for beatniking: 1. Like, a book of verse man. 2. A chick. 3. A BOTTLE OF SEAGRAM'S SEVEN. That was it. Seagram's Seven is liquor; you always drink it with 7 Up so you can ask at the bar for a 7 and 7. Reading the *Evergreen Review*s through from issue one, until it stopped, you can see how Madison Avenue encroached on the Village, and they were never very far apart. And the best you can say for that 'beatniking' is that you can have it.

Kelly and I went to some festival reception at the Commonwealth Pool. An Olympic-size swimming pool full of wine, or much more than enough. Kelly goes missing. This older woman comes up to me and says a very drunk Kelly is asking for me in the women's toilets. The older woman carries her out by her arms while her man takes her by the legs to carry her to their car. We'd had enough – nice of them though. En route to the car, at the same time, they both notice she's got no knickers on under her red mini skirt. The woman's frantically trying to pull down her skirt. But the boy on the ankles end can see right up the breakfast. She was sick in their car. They took us back to the student room with the sink in it.

I knew what crapulence was the next day. Shagging away in such a pitch of a hangover; culminating in a reversal of the senses I'd been looking for for a long time. I ate a shite off the floor. It appeared as pure gold to me.

It was a muggy day and she wanted to go out onto The Meadows to sunbathe. I say no it's not a good idea. She puts down on the grass too near the guys setting up the fair rides. One of them comes over and says, 'Whatever turns you on darling.' We can't have our scene to ourselves.

From time to time I see submissions for Jock's magazine. Don't want to see another story set in a pub, or starts, 'Two pints of heavy mate.' I hope you've done nowt like that Davie. That said though, an old guy came up to me, in a pub, and says to me like this, 'I sure hate drinking alone.'

'Me too,' I said. Turns out he was an American from Chicago – a Lutheran minister. He was with some sort of convention/pilgrimage. It seems St Giles in Edinburgh is as The Vatican to Lutherans. You don't meet many men of the cloth – I got right in amongst the issues. I said I'd met these hippies recently who believed that having 'good' thoughts stopped you from getting cancer. I'd said it was carcinogenic substances that caused cancer. 'Ah yes,' the minister said, 'and no one knows what these substances are.' He said he knew a lot of men of science who were also religious. He told about some particle physicists that had built a cyclotron, which was a huge underground tunnel 24 miles long. And that this tunnel generated the same power as a human sneeze. I realise – man I'm being sermonised here; that sneeze was contrived to blow my mind, along the lines of *ah the vanity of human wishes*, etc. He asked me where I stood in the matter of religion. Purely for mischief I said, 'I'm drawn towards the concept of Our Lady.'

'Ah Mary,' he said. 'Mary I don't mind at all – as long as Joseph can have equal billing.' You could tell he'd come out with that one before. It had that doctrinaire air.

I was reminded of the old surrealist story of how they made 'St Matthew's Martinis' by holding up the vermouth to sunlight letting the rays of sunlight then pass through the gin, like the Holy Ghost had passed through the virgin's hymen, leaving it intact as St Matthew had written.

I felt I could hardly speak to this Lutheran anymore. I wished I had bugs in my hair I could throw at him. Joseph was surely the most inconsequential boy in all the gospels;

only fit for pulling the donkey's nose along. Made a cuckold of by the Holy Ghost. Ars Theologia: Arse Theologia. I made my excuses and left Davie, aye.

It wouldn't have happened overnight, but it seems compressed in my mind. Kelly was this spiky-haired, gawky punk lassie with green drainpipes, bony knees sticking out. Then the hair grew and grew into dresses and mini skirts. One day she came out with the phrase, (used without irony), 'Us leggy model types'.

She met this girl at university who put her onto this camera club, in the back of Camera 4 on Howe St. You have a contact-sheet done in various states of undress down to 'full figure' or nude shots. Guys come in and look at a collection of these contact-sheets and pick a model to photograph, one guy or groups of guys. Tenner a shot to the girl. The changing rooms were downstairs and you had dusty feet by the time you'd walked from there onto the cardboard rollers used as backdrops. She did plenty of work and was gifted clothes and make-up. She even bought a bra which she'd never worn before.

She came to visit me at Bernard St. one night. Threw down this £20 on the bed. 'I stood under the statue of Rabbie Burns. The first car that stopped I asked the man for £15, but he said it was too much and drove off.' She said, 'I got in the back with the next guy. He came in the johnnie as soon as he got it in. Said it was the quickest tenner I'll ever make. He said he had a friend and I said I don't do anything kinky. But he said: No no nothing like that, I'll drive you out to the farmhouse and it'll be just him. It was like he said. His pal with these rough farmer's hands over me. He had a tiny cock. I'll have to get a shower.' She said the guy wanted to meet her the next night. We went to the pictures instead.

Kelly got her degree. Replying to an advert in the paper she was a double glazing salesperson in no time. She goes and knocks the doors, gets people interested . . . aye you know . . . Old Roy comes round later and gets them to sign. Teamwork. How was the parlance: Close the deal.

Roy took her to an Indian restaurant. The meal was lousy so they didn't leave much of a tip. The waiter helped her on with her coat saying, 'Your coat . . . yes, it's a very old one.' She said she made it with Roy back at his hotel in gratitude for the Indian meals. Apropos of nothing one day she comes out with, 'My Boss has got balls like tennis balls.'

'Did you suck his cock?'

'No, I'm sort of saving that up.'

The fat Essex man (you know him) king of porn rip-offs managed to get a licence from the council for two sex shops. One on Leith Walk, the other on Dalry Road. I had a job in them. A heavy guy came over from Glasgow to train me up, 'Now we're wanting the stuff going out the door. That's the main thing. Punter takes a magazine for £8 you take one from behind the counter here – they're crap, it's all crap. You give 'um, "We'll call it a tenner then big boy O.K." He takes two at £6 each; chuck in another one for £15. He takes two £8 ones; we'll call it the £20. See the principle? Fine. They've got a hard-on looking at all the magazines and they want offsky pronto. Don't let nobody take the shrink-wrapping off the magazines. The videos on the wall are £30. The ones down here, they're the right ones, they're £70. Only play the right ones through the lounge. The lounge is a fiver. You'll no want to go in there yourself, the spunk'll be fleein' about through there. I'm only jokin! Any bother phone me or Harry, got it? I'll sit with ye the day, see if yer any good an 'at.'

'What about the lingerie and dildos?'

'Nobody buys that stuff, but if any perverts do come in it's all marked. Throw in one of these wee crappy vibrators. Same as the magazines.'

So it was two or three days a week in the sex shop with Pete and Marie. Poor junkies, both dead now Davie, aye. The sex shop was a brief gig though. They started putting prostitutes' addresses and phone numbers (snap-shots in some cases) on a cork pin-board behind the till. The papers got hold of it and the council took away their licence.

Christopher and Brian wanted me to write a screenplay based on the Book of Job. They get this idea purely from they like Blake's illustrations for Job. I set to work in Old College library right away. This is the library at the top of the Mound, right under the armpit of John Knox's statue. It is the most serene place. I ate it up. I would walk from the sex shop to there. I read everything on the Book of Job. Even unto *The Proceedings of the Society of Dermatologists; Psychosomatic Dermatology* circa 4 BC (Job is smitten with a plague of boils). I made copious notes, and when I felt like it I'd just browse through the place. A good book was *The World's Bible: The Bible, The Koran, Gita, Vedas, Gilgamesh,* etc. A good book to have. I'll have to take a diversion here and say that when you have a kid Davie, be sure and teach it the value of comparative religion. There's no underestimating learning generally, but tolerance they should know.

I lived in Shepherd's Bush for a little while and it was just a little while I'll tell you: now Shepherd's Bush seemed to me like a vast council estate that feeds the BBC with workers. We had a make-up artist staying with us (the rest were unemployed actors) whose room was a shrine to a soft pack of Marlboros. She'd swiped them ages ago from David Bowie when he'd come to the BBC to do Brecht's *Baal*. She'd done his make-up. Everyone had gone out this night. I was left in the house with no fags and no fuck all. You can see it. I smoked them all. There were about two draws in each one . . . It only took until the next again day 'til she twigged and she lost it. She attacked me with a fork. Sausaged my ribs. She created such an atmosphere that it was impossible for me to stay. I left London. So Davie teach your kids they can fuck with anybody's god they feel like, but they should cover their arse and *always remember to replace the fags*.

Christopher, Brian and all their university/film school pals had been round a typewriter one night and had made this thing called a 'treatment'. They had *National Geographic*s out and typed out: We propose to shoot the film in India. We propose to shoot it in the desert. A point's system will apply for all the crew, etc. Brian's girlfriend had done a couple of drawings of costumes. They showed me this document. I said why don't you let me do it and put this in the bucket. They were offended that I wanted to put their sweated labour in the bucket. They hawked this treatment (which I thought should've included a synopsis of the actual film) around and eventually gave up on the whole thing when the Arts Council described it as illiterate.

The pain Davie, the 'toothache' in the baws. I'm going to have a look at your MS now: I thought it was a novel, but it's a sheaf of short stories. I'll pick out the first one.

*   *   *

Mr Archibald was blind. Most Sundays he would go out walking under the patient care of his guide dog, Lucky. Mr Archibald had had the golden lab' for seven years. This particular Sunday had been the fairest for weeks and after his Three O'Clock sherry, man and dog took a pleasant walk on Queen's Drive; a well-paved road that runs by the palace of Holyrood House. A gentle wind blew ripples on St Margaret's Loch and displaced Mr Archibald's thinning hair. He stopped in his tracks as he heard Lucky bark. The dog struggled and broke from him. He thought perhaps Lucky had gone up Arthur's Seat after a rabbit, but was distressed as this was contrary to his training and an unique occurrence. Whistling and calling heel he slapped the ground with his steel cane. In a short while a policeman came by and raised the alarm, but the dog was nowhere to be seen. Lucky ran and ran until finally he paused whimpering and shaking on top of the crags at Arthur's Seat. In a second he leapt straight over the edge and dropped down the two hundred feet.

Elizabeth and Billy were walking to school. 'Have you seen the "Emperor's Warriors" yet?' asked Billy.

'No. What's that?'

'Exhibit at the City Art Centre. Good grief. Like it's been on the telly and everywhere.'

'Yeah? Well we've been settled in for a couple of weeks already, but we haven't got a t.v. yet.'

Elizabeth knew all about how to make contact with a new city and had started talking to Billy the first day at school, after she'd overheard him talking in the staffroom. He was the youngest teacher at the school.

'You manipulate that cigarette in your mouth like a tough little Nelson Algren character,' she'd said to him.

'What? . . . Now he was a New Yorker like yourself wasn't he?'

'How d'you know where I come from?'

'Everybody knows. You're a celebrity.'

'My God. Is that so? No, he's Chicago I think.'

From this first exchange, Liz and Billy walked to school together most days. Liz'd been worried at first that the way Billy talked had been calculated for her benefit. Condescending flags of welcome. But she soon found out nearly all the kids used U.S. phrases from time to time.

Liz'd come over from New York with her friend Aimy to share a flat together in Edinburgh. They'd met at the co-operative, well-woman type clinic in New York where Aimy had practised. Aimy'd originally come from Edinburgh. In N.Y. Liz'd had an ex-boyfriend of hers marry Aimy so's she wouldn't get deported. Aimy'd had the opportunity to do research back in Edinburgh and to work at the Sick Children's Hospital, while Liz taught at the little school.

Liz and Tom clicked with books. They talked about Paul Bowles and Hubert Selby. Liz knew a girl who baby-sat for Kurt Vonnegut and Liz'd been to his house and'd met him. Billy knew a great-grand-daughter of Yeats's. Quite quickly they'd done with the name-dropping and favourite films. As they walked to school, Liz recalled how at first, Billy thought she was a lesbian and how they'd had a good laugh when she'd told him she lived with her gynaecologist. She thought that from book talk on towards Billy's bedroom, in stages of a casual pace, had been a natural progression for like-minded boys and girls. Not that there was anything uneasy in the first place, it had somehow cleared the air. The crisp Autumn morning gave rise to happy thoughts about herself and her life. She'd bought a new outfit that weekend. The clothes felt stiff and fresh. Not feeling much like talking, she listened in to the unfamiliar swish of her underskirt. Billy said she looked 'schoolmistressy', though she still wore sportshoes, carrying heels for class in a leather handbag.

Tom and Liz turned a corner and school faced them at the bottom of a long avenue which led down into Edinburgh's Southside. The road was busy with parents driving their children to school – some fancy cars, Liz had noted on her first week, though a handful of well wrapped-up kids did pass them on foot. The school building was a two storey affair of newly blasted sandstone, with high 1920's windows which were being washed.

'They're getting it ready for us Billy.'

'How about we go to this exhibition then, this afternoon? Seeing as we've the half-day.'

'O.K. Sure. I'll see you at half 'one.'

As they walked across the playground, she warmed to the bustle of the children's play. A little blonde girl flashed her a brilliant smile, 'Good morning Miss Straus.'

In school, Liz put her heels on and did up her long dark hair with kirbys. As she took her spectacle case from her coat pocket the bell rang. First thing on a Monday was a double period of English. She entered the class and the pupils' chatter soon abated. They all stood and chorused their 'Good morning' in unison. After the usual banging of desk lids and scraping of chairs the lesson began. 'Now. Listen up you guys. I do hope you've all done your composition homework. Miss Gray, yes you on the left, Sally, what was our topic?'

'A Description of Nature miss.'

'Correct.'

Sally Gray read out her homework and the lesson went on with each taking their turn to read out. '. . . We saw a tree and it was silver and it was skinnier than all the other trees in the forest. It had hundreds of birds' nests in it, but my Uncle Andy said it was a disease . . .'

'I'm sorry I'm late miss.' A boy who seemed rather taller than anyone in the class stood by the door. He wore no coat but only a woollen Fair Isle pullover, worn jeans and tennis shoes. His hair was longish and damp-looking. Over his shoulder was slung a canvas satchel. 'Come in Barclaye. You're late. Again.' There was an element of the ironic aside to the class in Liz's tone, but she was genuinely annoyed. A smart little boy called Jamie sniggered at the back of the class. Barclaye took a vacant desk beside him. 'You're stinking. You've *had* it.' Liz asked him if he'd done his homework. 'Oh miss no. I forgot. Honest. I just couldn't get a minute to do it.'

'Then Mr Barclaye Reid, I must insist that you stay behind at the conclusion of this lesson.' Anger made her address the pupils in an overly formal manner, and she never needed any more than this to produce acceptable behaviour. This Barclaye Reid though was beginning to perplex her.

She'd had complaints about Barclaye's habitual lateness from Mr Galbraith, the fat history teacher. Mr Galbraith had a huge, wet bottom lip and swayed back and forward on the balls of his feet as he talked. He gesticulated wildly with his arms as if he'd been about to grapple Liz at any moment. She hated his guts. Galbraith had talked about how he'd love to 'melt' Barclaye and he'd told her to be sure and send him along to him should he be late again.

As the class left after the lesson, Liz summoned Barclaye to stand by the blackboard. He slouched against it, crossing his legs at the ankles. She was struck by his hands: The long fingernails and the two rings of a cheap metal which had rubbed off verdigris at the base of his fingers. 'Why are you always late Barclaye?'

'I don't know miss, I left the house in plenty time.'

'How far from school do you live?'

'Oh, quite far, but not very very far.'

'But you're consistently late, now how can this be? Do you want me to send you to Mr Galbraith?'

'No miss.'

'And what about your parents?'

'My father's dead. My mum's a cleaner at The Commonwealth Pool.' Liz sighed and felt her face redden a little. 'Well I guess I'll have to have a word with her.' Barclaye didn't seem at all put out and said, 'O.K. miss. O.K. She finishes at two.'

From the car park at the back of the school, Barclaye led her over some busy roads and through side-streets behind terraced houses. They walked over a weedy patch of open ground until they paused for a while on stone steps which led down a slope into a park. There wasn't a soul about. Liz was impressed with her first, close at hand view of Arthur's Seat. Somehow she'd expected there to be a fence around it, but there was none. She thought it looked like a huge volcanic stump like you see in the desert in westerns, except here there was grass around the slopes. Behind the plug that made up the sheer crags lay a rugged area of green peaks and valleys. The highlands on your doorstep.

Barclaye was excited, trying to take everything in by whirling round on the spot, 'This is a short-cut miss,' he said and they went down the steps into the park. As they passed a little grove of elm trees he said, 'You see that building there miss? Through the trees? Behind that wall? That's a brewery that's connected with an underground tunnel that goes right away up to Arthur's Seat miss. I've been right along it but it's boarded-up now. Once when I was out picking mushrooms in the shadow of the brewery wall, a huge rat came out at me from under a pile of grain. That was the day my big brother Murray said they were for soup for the boys in Saughton Jail miss. The boys like their soup up there, no kidding, because my brother came back drunk late that night miss and he woke me up and gave me a fiver.'

They came onto the pavement that rings around the base of Arthur's Seat and by the loch known as St Margaret's. 'That's where The Queen lives over there,' Barclaye said, pointing to Holyrood House.

'Why do they call it Arthur's Seat Barclaye?' asked Liz then wished she hadn't.

'I've really no idea. Mallard ducks, some teal and tufted ducks on the pond. Over the crags is Duddingston Loch though miss, much better for nesting. Miles of reed and marshy ground. Woods as well.'

'Oh Barclaye, you steal birds' eggs?'

'Not at this time of year miss, April or May's best for

nesting. You get ducks, waterhens, coots, pied wagtails, even terns nested there one year. They built nests, wove little platforms low in the reeds but didn't lay any eggs. Terns are sea-birds really. Once we saw a heron's nest but we couldn't get to it. You get every kind of goose at Duddingston Loch as well, but they don't nest, they just come here in the winter.'

'I sort of get the idea you come here a lot.'

'I'm here all the time miss.'

The pavement became steep and curved up round the hill. Liz followed as Barclaye broke from the pavement and tramped up a path between what seemed a forest of gorse bushes. 'I thought . . . it sounded like a curlew there,' she said.

'No miss,' Barclaye said shyly. 'That was starlings. Starlings can make the noise of any bird.' Liz thought she'd better not say any more.

As they pushed on, on an upward track through rough grass, the sun broke and sent a slow-moving wave up the hill. Liz found that she still had her heels on and had left her sportshoes at school. After a few more yards, she stopped at some withered stalks of lupins that had curled like ferns. She took her shoes off and her feet felt cool on the dry, springy grass. Looking over Leith and out to the sea, she felt dizzy to think she was so high up. To stabilise herself she looked at the ground, then gestured to Barclaye and pointed to some black pearls among the grass.

'Pellets miss,' he said.

'Pellets?'

'*Rabbits'* pellets miss.'

'Oh.' Liz carried her shoes regardless, and soon there

was no path at all. Barclaye was headed in the direction of the crags. As high as they could go, they came to a small gully that wasn't many yards from the edge of the crags. 'Stand still,' said Barclaye and thoroughly inspected the grass all around them. 'I don't see any rabbits' stuff around here,' said Liz.

'There's no animals here, not mice nor voles or anything miss.'

The gully seemed a lovely, secluded spot and as they walked down into it, Liz noticed there was no breeze and everything was still. There wasn't the slightest track here. Barclaye was picking his way carefully between certain clumps of grass, certain flat stones. Liz kept directly behind him. Looking in the grass, she saw feathers to the left and right, almost in a uniform pattern. The feathers were about three inches long, light grey with a single red spot ¾ way along the shaft. 'You've got to watch up here miss, people fall off the crags all the time, three or four last year.'

They were on the upward slope and nearly out of the gully, when Barclaye knelt and parted a veil of hanging moss. Liz knelt beside him. He exposed a little cave shut over with three pieces of slate, each cut in a cone shape. Very delicately he removed slates behind which were seventeen little coffins, two tiers of eight and one starting a third tier. The coffins were about as long as a dialing finger and an inch wide. He lifted out the top-most coffin. It had incredibly fine tin ornaments placed regularly over the lid and sides. He lifted off the lid and inside was a little man made of wood, fully dressed in fine-fitting burial clothes with sleeves and trousers. His facial features were perfectly formed as if he could speak, his eyes closed, his cheeks slightly puffed. Barclaye brought out another coffin and inside was another little man. Though the wood was older, it appeared this was a younger person. Most of the coffins on the bottom tier looked badly decayed but the one on top had obviously been placed there quite recently. Liz felt she shouldn't touch them, but without saying anything, Barclaye showed her six of the figures, all of them individually dressed and each with their own distinctive facial features. Seeing that everything was as it had been, Barclaye put the slates back and closed the cave over.

Liz followed Barclaye's measured tread in silence away from the gully. Taking a southward path down, they came onto a road and Duddingston Loch came into view. It was quite late now and the light seemed thinner. She had a vague, not unpleasant feeling of being tricked. They sat on a bench together.

'Well . . . we're late,' said Liz, bursting out laughing.

'D'you fancy a fag miss?' said Barclaye, offering her one.

'A fag!' She giggled uncontrollably and lit them up from a lighter in her shoe. Barclaye laughed as well.

'I've never seen anything like those little men,' she said, putting on her shoes and trying to replace kirby grips. Her head tilted back and she saw the clear blue sky above her, empty but for a single white vapour trail. 'You know, they didn't look human those little men, maybe they're the effigies of little extra-terrestrials . . .' she said, nodding towards the sky.

'Well, whatever. I hope you'll not be taking today's route to school in future.'

Barclaye was quiet for a minute.

'I'll try not to be late again miss. Would you like me to walk you home?'

'Thanks, but I'm sure I'll be able to find my way from here.'

They said goodbye and she took the road down to the bottom of Arthur's Seat. From the pavement she looked back and saw him up on the hill as if he was checking she'd be all right.

Well that's an attempt at a varnished tale Davie lad. Wee bit quality lit'. I was wondering where those photocopies I made from *The Proceedings of the Society of Scottish Antiquarians* had gone. I must've sent them to you because I know that one of them was about those wee coffins. The old antiquarians didn't know what to make of them. I had a loose theory which I'm glad I didn't tell you. It was when whaling ships left from Leith, there was always a service at St Mary's Chapel on Arthur's Seat to pray for the safe return of the men. And that after this service, should there've been any man lost at sea since the last service, he was buried in tiny effigy at a secret mass tomb on Arthur's Seat. That was a bit cheeky of you there though, anyway it's an old-fashioned story.

She's away with it all though Davie. I've no papers, letters, Fuji standard 8 in green reels. Reels and reels. Shots of the flat fields and copse land around Oxford. Getting a flat in Oxford was easy. At first I just stayed in an hotel. Last pint with the landlord at the bar. Up at 8.30 for breakfast, usually kippers. 100 minute bus at the market in the car park. Into Victoria, swift walk in the green park before Picadilly and the West End. Back for tea-time to Oxford, to the Banbury

Road. All the arseholes on the bus in, checking *The Guardian* media pages for jobs.

Sunday walks along the meandering Isis. I remember it in Fuji colour – a startled duck, its tail cutting away since from the sluice gate and up into the sky. Kelly by the bank in a tartan coat. A milk vending machine in the street. The bookshops. I'll come to the bookshops later. As I said it was easy to get a flat. The woman in the agents said, 'Go and see this flat, you'll definitely get it you will. First white face we've seen today.' The flat was above the Central TV studios, across the street from the Museum of Modern Art.

At this time I was at, what I called then, the work of the soft pencil. 2nd hand books. Edinburgh to Oxford and vice-versa. It's easy to learn what's under-priced and what will sell. Edinburgh bought old natural history, or technical books, and books on Scottish subjects. Oxford bought art, poetry, occult. A good score was a copy of *Lautremont*; a big book with the text like a postage stamp in the middle of the page, twelve colour Dali plates. I loved the Singen, sorry St-John Perse French/English text in the beautiful Bollingen Editions. Many more. 8 Poems by W.B. Yeats illustrated by Austin Spare, valuable as it was published in 1916 (a big deal for Yeatsophiles) but by far the best score of all was a very slim volume of poems by Paul Eluard translated by Samuel Beckett.

Michael Markovsky was given to inappopriate outbursts of rage or despair. Davie the boy was mental as you know. Transported from his native Poland, Michael's father had survived being a work slave for the Nazis in Czechoslovakia. After being liberated, and after months of marching, he got a ship bound for Glasgow where he met Michael's mum, an Irish woman. Now you can't go for any of those 'national types' generalities but for sure in Michael's case this Polish/Irish mix was genetic rocket fuel.

Michael had been in Oxford (Jesus College) at the same time as me but we didn't meet until later, I was 23, he was 25 and already had had a heart attack and burst piles. He'd wiped the floor with the Shetland fiddlers at drinking. You were impressed. He was on his 3rd university having matriculated at Aberdeen, disappearing with the grant money. Here at Edinburgh he was studying Sanskrit in a class of 2. He moaned that he had a complete set of *Chapman* (a local Qual' lit' periodical) but none of the Edinburgh bookshops would take them. I told him to try Oxford and he explained he couldn't really go back there.

At first we hung with like this Polish group at Gayfield Sq., drinking vodka and smoking opium; an unusual combination you might think. The White Night was never whiter, or in my case never whiteyer. Michael was a great man for wine though so we cooled out the Poles, and started drinking claret. He told me that from his house in the High St., David Hume would wave to Adam Smith across the Firth of Forth in Kirkcaldy. One of those stories you might think but I liked it. It gave me an insight into Oor Davie Davie. A man all of Edinburgh loved, but some people wouldn't get on with him because he didn't believe in god.

Michael knew I was trying to write at this time and took me to some parties where literary people were at. I never met any literary people. I remember one guy in a bow tie glowering at me as I tossed peanuts at his young son who was having great fun snapping at them like a dog. Michael and I are in the living room. A piece of cheese cake falls on the floor in the kitchen. 'Sorry you'll have to leave,' said a girl.

He would never get on too well with the girls that were around. It wasn't the specs or his missing front tooth; I think it was vegetarianism. He'd always be reminding me that, ounce for ounce peanuts had more protein than fillet steak. But the wash of peanut detritus past the missing tooth and into the wine glass disgust you if you weren't used to it. He usually had some career girlfriend tucked away somewhere who was mostly issuing ultimatums to him to get his act together.

He had his phases. He'd come round and say, 'Got the price of a pint?' and I'd say no just out of not wanting to go out. We'd talk or he'd help with notes on Alexis St-Léger Léger's *Oiseaux*. He had eight languages fully and was very handy for that sort of thing. He came round one day when I was living with Kelly. She and he were old mates from Glasgow. So he outs with, 'Got the price of . . . ?' to meet with honest denials. He goes and is back in half an hour with twelve bottles of assorted, good wines. Game on. He goes out later with an old broken typewriter of mine and is soon back with draw. The three of us have one tremendous high old time. Like out of nothing. The next again day Davie I cannot believe what she says, 'That Michael Markovsky is a bad yin, you should pay him off (Glasgow for sling him a deafy, ignore or get rid of). What if he phones us up and asks for bail or something?'

I learned a little about wine from him. Like Rioja we never drank – C18th claret heads man! But this day we had a few expensive bottles with the gold wire round them. We go round to see Johnny Ram from Yorkshire who is an intense fellow. He is doing his Ph.D. on Wyndham Lewis and spends all day listening to Fall records. He had all these theories about how the Fall guy was the Wyndham Lewis of nowadays (thenadays); intricate theories, devious, unconvincing. Michael said that in Kathy Acker's book she said she wanted to sleep with one of the Fall, so she needs the contact lenses right enough. Did you meet Johnny Ram Davie? He went missing not long after this.

I knew next to nothing about Logical Posivitism, but I'd heard it was an 'uncool, cold war philosophy'. (This from a guy that taught Froggy lit' crit'.) So when Michael told me Alfred Ayer, the father of Logical Posivitism, was coming to speak at the David Hume Tower and on David Hume, we decided to go. Michael and Alfred Ayer being both old Oxford men. Of his talk I remember little except that it was couched in a gentle, winning English. I'd've had to've been a philosopher of years' study, just to define his terms (to this day I haven't made a start on the study of Ethics Davie, perhaps I never shall). I do remember being deep into Non Aristotelean semantics, or I had a few of Korzybski's books on the subject. I was thinking about these, lulled by Freddie's honeyed tones. Suddenly I became aware of this embarrassing silence. The question and answer part of the lecture was producing not a word from the benches. I was embarrassed for Sir Freddie and it seemed we were being rude. Never mind, I thought, soon someone will speak. But it was going on and on. I became aware of my feet pressing inside my shoes, which I thought was toe-curling. But I was up, 'Sir, what would you have to say about the Non Aristotelean semantics of Count Alfred Korzybski?'

'What has this to do with my paper?'

Davie I wouldn't have been bothered about telling him nowadays I couldn't understand his fucking paper. 'Eh sir it's philosophy . . . em language.' I sat down. I could've crawled in beside the matches in my pocket.

'Korzybski, good heaven's I haven't heard his name since the 1930's. Of course he was a good *popular* writer . . .' I could tell that a *popular* writer was the ultimate put-down from a philosopher. But I had cracked the ice and he soon had questions from people who had heard him speak in the 1960's. Fans; from when he was a popular writer. You couldn't help but warm a bit to Sir Freddie when he asked, clearly looking for sport, 'Any Tories in the assembled company?' and not a peep.

The old Moral Philosophy chestnut of abortion came up. Sir Freddie states his view that it is the woman's right to terminate up to 28 days. Instantly Michael is up to his feet. 'Ah Korzybski' says Sir Freddie. 'No a colleague. Anyway how the fuck can you say that? 28 days? Naw, nae days. Nae abortions. Life's sacred man. Life's fucking sacred.' Michael went purple. Sir Freddie unfazed, cut Michael and was answering another question smoothly as we left.

We go right into The Pear Tree. I'm wondering: How can I have had Michael for such a David Hume man. Then he ups and gets so worked up about the archaic edicts of Rome? Davie it must've been that genetic rocket fuel I mentioned above. We have a few vodkas and black coffees, which Michael calls Polish coffees. Soon he is proposing a toast: Long live Poland. Viva Polska. Fuck Jaruzelski. Tanks back to the Volga! I'm not perplexed by any contradiction in people nowadays, but I was that day.

Soon after this Michael went away to Portugal. It was a language he knew and he made off with some grant or other.

After Oxford/Edinburgh I lived with Paul O'Malley in Garnethill. The Chinatown of Glasgow. He lived high up, across from the Chinese primary school. What a din the kids made in the playground practising for Chinese new year, running around with the big lion's head on, banging drums and cymbals.

Paul O'Malley went out with Kelly's younger sister Carol-Ann. Carol-Ann was one trendy miss at all times. She worked in clothes shops and the fashionable Enclave – a restaurant in the west end where Paul was a waiter. I remember the night Harry, Paul's boss, brought back the first crate of mescal seen in Scotland. I remember the desk sergeant the next again day saying to us, 'Mind ae callin me a poof last night?' Kelly told me about making it with Harry and his colostomy bag bursting on her.

There was a TV at Garnethill but no one watched it. We'd get up and have breakfast in the Equui cafe; always sitting in the back seat with all the names scored in the wood. This was around the beginning of the cappuccino days. I would trot out what I'd say every day, 'I have a date at Parnassus,' and along the road to Charing Cross and the Mitchell library. Kelly would be off through to Edinburgh to Napier (then) College.

We'd rendezvous back at Garnethill for tea-time and eat something bought out Henry Healy's (a Glasgow deli). In the evenings we'd go wherever the theatre with concessions was at, either across the bridge to the Citizens' or the drama school at Buchanan St. There was always the pictures. The film *Diva* had a big effect on Kelly. I thought it was pretentious French shite. One weekend we saw *Gone With the Wind* on a Saturday and *All the President's Men* (the Watergate story with Hoffman and Redford as Woodward and Bernstein) the next night. Kelly decided that all along she'd wanted to be a journalist, a crusader. And inspired by Vivien Leigh in the fields, she wasn't going to be 'poor' anymore. Davie were you sure I was to spare you nothing? I'd forgotten about all of this. Soon I was being dragged to The Opera. 'You've got to get a new jacket. A *designer* jacket.' I made do with some second hand affair (still smart like). I'm sure the keen eye would've been able to tell, but to me it looked the same as that scarecrow-style Cath Hamnett.

Some opera I must confess was all right. Five acts with three intervals scuppered me a bit though. We had a row before the fifth act of *Aida*, 'No fuck it. I'm staying at the bar.' You could still see and hear from there. Lovely pyramid sets and that. My favourite was *The Magic Flute* though, and Weber's *Oberon* I liked – just because Anthony Burgess was the librettist. Your Zucchinis and Tortellinis you could keep.

To be nearer Napier, Kelly took a flat at Henderson Row, above Jock Gillies' bar. She was deep in hero-worship of some guy Bill who ran the journalism course. 'Bill said ... Bill said ...' Bill said that in reporting, the reporter must bring the bear directly onto the stage. Nice one Bill. I rented a TV and video for the flat and moved in. I checked with the course books: *Power without Responsibility*, *Teeline* – had a bash at trying to learn the shorthand and then thought, *What* am I doing? Also lying around were; *A History of Obscenity Trials* (old hat to us remember), *Index on Censorship*, *New Internationalist*, *Police Review*, and heaven help us, a subscription to *Granta*.

Round this time I was in with a very handy boy called Max Jarvie. Maxie. The Man The Bookies Fear. He looked after difficult teenagers at this time. But had been previously living on the Isle of Man, organising god knows what, all to do with horse racing, an off-shore concern. I was nearly in love with Maxie and god bless anyone that can take money off the bookmakers. Anyway bookies know it's good for business if occasionally, someone is seen going out the shop with money. Even though Maxie kept his hand in a little horses, money was not his god. 'I hate these race-track Johnnies,' he'd say. 'Race trackers with their "holding and folding – that's what it's all about" arseholes.' If Maxie knew a horse, he'd tell me and it'd win. Funny thing 6/1 always seemed to be the magic price, not too greedy but still more than worthwhile. Maxie's wife was Alison. She was great. Her and Maxie were back from this holiday in Paris and she said to me like this, 'You know, Maxie this is right though eh, it was that cold at the top of the Eiffel Tower, that cold, that I had to wear *two* jerseys.'

'No one in Fleet St. will be able to collect a pay packet under the name Mickey Mouse anymore.' I'm having explained to me the terrible abuses perpetrated by the print-workers. That and New Technology, Eddie Shah's *Today*, Wapping, and hey, colour pictures. 'Two detectives came to check the toilets in the afternoon. You know when Princess Anne eats a baked potato, she only eats the skin and leaves the rest.' A scoop. Kelly's doing a little off-hand waitressing at this time.

I taped this TV programme, *At the Edge of the Union*, a documentary about Northern Ireland. It showed the day to day lives of Peter Robinson and Martin McGuiness. The BBC banned its showing until they could restore 'balance' to it by adding ten seconds of a parked car being blown up. Their tampering sticks out like a sore thumb. Kelly took the tape to college. It's still part of the course materials.

She had another boyfriend at this time. A chef. He broke into her house one night. He was there when she came in. He'd made himself a joint. She wanted him to go home. She managed this because, she said, 'It's easy to manipulate people when they're stoned.'

In your last there Davie you were asking what drugs am I into nowadays? Well a few weeks ago I was going along Albert St.

(mind it used to be called 'scag alley'). This young boy comes up to me and says 'Wantin' any dee effs? A pound.'

'No man I'm just into Ecky and blaw.'

'Aye, for the come down then?'

'No man. They do yer guts in. Cheers.' And that was it. Albert St. though. Allan Ramsey, he's got a ground floor flat in Albert St. Came in from his work one day and christ his house has been robbed. He was devastated, he went right away into The Clan for a drink. He was having his pint and trying to straighten himself out when a guy tried to sell him his duvet cover.

Me and Cicely have been doing some taping. You've never met her Davie, but if it wasn't for her and well, you (don't get embarrassed) there were no warm-blooded people left in the world. A transcription of the tape was going to be in Jock's magazine, but it never appeared. John Berryman was a great poet and was a best mate of Delmore Schwartz. You'll know his name from your shitey old Velvets records.

TAPE ON

CICELY: I'm interested in John Berryman; you were talking about Berryman there.

ME: Well I just like Berryman y'know separate from those other Middle Poets he gets lumped in with eh Lowell, Stevens and all that Boston confession/depression thing. What's Berryman's line, I can't remember it all, 'De dum de dum de dum . . . Voice of a lost soul moving . . .' That's great. (pause) He has to mark a poem by one of his students about a guy that throws himself off a bridge in St Paul's,

Minneapolis. This exact bridge is walking distance from where Berryman is teaching. Berryman jumps off the bridge to his death the next again day, like suggested by his student's poem. Maybe that's not such a big deal though. It seems depressives are in a highly suggestible state as Styron says in his book about his depression – he couldn't look at a tree without seeing a noose hanging from it. So maybe . . .

CICELY: William Styron would be depressed because he's such a fuckin shite writer.

ME: Hey now.

CICELY: Well, *Sophie's Choice* – I ask you. Anyway, Berryman; he was very well thought of in the 'sixties right?

ME: I think it was 1974 he topped himself. Of course he wasn't a great counter-culture man, didn't think much of Bob Dylan or Ginsberg who certainly took from him . . . Yea, like his diary tells of a lecture tour he did all over the states in 1969, 'Tonight after my lecture I was offered three different kinds of marijuana by students, these I refused . . .' Well.

CICELY: He ought to've taken the draw right?

ME: Well, yea, rather than the whisky and barbiturates.

CICELY: Three different kinds?

ME: Aye. In these dry times it makes your lips stick together to think of it eh . . . Ye gums and resinous woods thereof! The real Cedars of Lebanon! (pause) I don't like opiates, barbiturates, prescribed drugs generally and fucking especially I don't like cocaine.

CICELY: I'll tell you – cocaine people are really dripping with money to the point it's mad. I baby-sat once for this girl who was right into coke. She came round and offered me £50 and a lump of draw like a cricket-ball to baby-sit for her so I said eh all right. So it's me, Val and this girl in her big house all blowing away, and the idea is that I sit tight while Val and the girl go to a club – except it's getting later and later and they're not going anywhere. I start to get drowsy and the last thing I remember is being asked if I want anything to eat. Next thing I know I'm coming round and here's this smell coming from boxes stacked up and the girl says, 'We didn't want to wake you up to find out what sort of pizza you wanted, so we got you these.' Fucking eight different kinds of pizza. Picked the pineapple off of one for dessert. Crazy. Never saw a kid . . .

ME: Well, regardless of the people around it, coke's a horrible drug though. I remember in an Italian restaurant, after shutting, we were playing cards for lines, and I remember the chef winning all the lines. He takes out this little hard cock, rubs coke all over the end of it and running at the wall, he goes, 'Look! I am so stoned! I fuck the wall!' He was an' all – making dents in the hessian. Christ's sake.

CICELY: Enough of that . . . So Berryman, he was altogether more with the juicers, Dylan Thomas and that?

ME: See that's just the thing though. When you look into it, Berryman's two most loved poets, the ones who influenced him the most were Baudelaire and Yeats right. Now Baudelaire wrote a great piece, 'Poème du Hashish' which is like more like an essay where he describes a young Parisian 1850's style, who, determined to take hashish for the first time, goes to an Arab cafe. It seems you dropped your bit wrapped in a vine leaf and downed it with coffee. So the young guy does this and . . . Baudelaire goes to great lengths describing the guy's queasiness and creeping terror in the streets. Eventually he goes into a pharmacy and explains to the pharmacist he's been taking hashish and must have a cure. The pharmacist offers to shout for the gendarmes right away if he doesn't get out of his shop. It's very funny, a totally ad absurdum piece like De Quincey's 'On Murder Considered as One of the Fine Arts'.

CICELY: Like a shaggy dog story?

ME: Yea, even. Baudelaire wrote a great deal on hashish; I mean on and about. That whole artificial paradise thing and a collection with Gautier, *Hashish*, *Wine*, *Opium*, a thorough study of all three. It's just . . . you'd've thought Berryman could've demonstrated a bit more curiosity.

CICELY: What about Yeats though?

ME: Well we know that Yeats was blowing away in Paris with followers of the C18th mystic Saint-Martin, about 40 years after Baudelaire. It's in 'The Trembling of the Veil'. He's taking it at 'One in the morning and some are dancing.'

CICELY: Yea that's a good title, '. . . and some are dancing'.

ME: So even Yeats there. If he'd moved to Paris and cultivated sticky lips from the 1890's onwards, maybe his eyes wouldn't have got so bad.

CICELY: 'Dear Ms Gonne too stoned to write you last month . . .' (laughs).

ME: (laughs) Poor cunt Berryman though. When I think of it.

CICELY: Thinking! Now ye start!

ME: No no. When I think of it, Berryman, his father committing suicide and all, it's like . . . The bonfire was always waiting at the end of the road. His particular bonfire. What he connected with in Baudelaire was suffering, guilt.

CICELY: And rather than mysticism or hashish, from Yeats he got what? . . . lyricism?

ME: Aye, the wind blowing in the reeds, nae doubt.

CICELY: So you told me you're not into this and that drug. What about Ecky?

ME: Well I think I've only had it the once that was really, really good; at a club in Glasgow, Jesus Christ I thought I was in a cathedral made out of glacier mints. Somehow this cool, blue European thing was blasting through me. I thought I was in Iceland and Berlin at the same time. Nothing like that since. What about your Cis?

CICELY: I just cannot take anything hallucinogenic at all now. Know what I mean, *Quelle barbe*! what a bore. It was . . . I just heard too much shit talked around me. The slightest profundity made me sick. I like a blow and maybe a glass of wine.

ME: And good sounds right?

CICELY: Right. Some of us are dancing!

ME: I sort of see what you mean about the acid though. I've seen people take acid too young, too much too young, and they develop . . . what can I tell you . . . a taste for introspection that might not've been in their character.

CICELY: Did you read Marcuse?

ME: Nut.

CICELY: He was promoting LSD as about to bring about a world revolution, starting in the streets of Paris in 1968. He was a Marxist, totally separate from Leary and Kesey and that.

ME: Sounds like that, 'Surrealism in the Service of the Revolution' but surrealism wouldn't serve. Wouldn't serve brussel sprout ... Nah the last thing I want to say about hallucinogens is well ... I got this science book, *Inspection By Torchlight*. It's about spectral analysis which tells that colours have their own rhythms; a blue rhythm is at the opposite end of the spectrum from a red rhythm – every colour in-between has its own rhythm. André Michaux, the painter, wrote this book called *Rhythms of Vision*, it's about his experiments with mescalin. He has these drawings in this book identical to spectral analysis charts. Old André is just drawing what he sees. Nothing poetic in that.

CICELY: A poetic statement needs must be unscientific?

ME: Well unfortunately that's what people seem to expect. Eh ... when the scientific community want to dismiss someone their thought is called 'poetic', Reich for example.

CICELY: Sure we don't deal with no scientific community, or for that matter any religion.

ME: Fucking right man. Science-religion, religion-science – two cheeks of the same ugly arse.

TAPE ENDS

I remained in Edinburgh while Kelly moved to Stirling. She was reporting for *The Alloa and Hillfoots Advertiser*. I'd go through to Stirling from time to time. Take one or two pictures for the paper. I remember the old editor guy telling me, 'Aye the paper used to be all poems. All poems.' Hugh MacDiarmid had been the editor. If I didn't go through to Stirling I'd get a phone call such as, 'You better have the money for my driving lessons.' When I was in Stirling though, a lawyer guy or this South African photographer would knock at the door; they'd be told, 'No you can't come in just now, my friend's here.' Then to me, 'Aye right enough that guy's got a fancy for me.' Half smiling.

I was being Contact 400ed at this time. She'd say, 'Got any tips for the horses? Got any jokes? Got any dope? What have you *got*?' This was all to pass on to be one of the guys in the office. She started moonlighting on *The Sun* and was soon full-time. She loved to boast about the great spoilers that 'we' did on the *Daily Record*. 'You don't like what I do,' she said. 'You're fucking right.' I stopped going through to Stirling.

A few weeks later a guy comes up to me when I'm out in Edinburgh and says to me like this, 'Your fucking girlfriend's lost me my job. I had a good job there managing that restaurant. She said we were having orgies when it was shut. Pish. Got me the sack.' A wee lassie comes up to me this other night, 'Your fucking girlfriend . . .'

'She's no my girlfriend.'

'Anyway that lassie keeps chapping at my mate's door. There's a rumour going round that my mate's shagged Simon Le Bon. She's up at her house all the time shouting through the letter box. My mate can't go out or anything.'

People like to carry news to me about Kelly. To see if I give a fuck. I give less than a fuck. She's the city editor of

The Sun last I heard. You saw her byline right under *your money* Davie. Christopher, Brian and Michael Markovsky met her in The City Cafe recently. They were reminiscing about their university days. She said that it was funny how out of all of them she was the only one still doing what she'd studied. Like Brian was a science administrator now. Christopher was a computer guy. Michael was a cab driver. Michael asked her, 'What was it you did at university again?' and she said, '*English Literature*.'

Davie that was the biggest laugh. Biggest laugh them three guys ever had anyhow.

Remember Maurice? When you knew him he was one of those fellows always on the phone, shifting money about for a living. I remember he mad about this Italian girl. People were fed up of him going on about her. He did the whole football bus once, eventually sitting next to me, 'Italian lassies are the best shag eh?' And on about how when she'd visit, she be pulling him into public toilets and all this. Well he moved to Verona. Learned Italian so that he'd get on with the lassie's folks. He got a job editing a newspaper in Verona. He phoned me up the other day from his new job at the Vatican. Aye Maurice edits the newspaper of the Vatican city. He told me how he went to interview Franco Zeffirelli. He'd had these huge hounds at his dinner table and he'd launch steaks at them for them to snap at. When Maurice was on the phone, I asked him what was that weird sound coming through from the background. He said, 'Bells'.

Young Kenneth still keeps the faith at all times. He gets his three months out for his field study for a masters degree in anthropology. He's off to study naturists in Sweden and France. Says nudists are a tribe like any other, and will break down into all the disciplines. Speaking of discipline he says he's writing a vegetarian S & M book called 'Strict Vegetarians'.

My burns have been getting better over the course of it. I even tried to watch television the other night. I put it on, and what do I hear except, '1984: is it the past? or is it the future?' Aye Davie it's definitely the past. Thank fuck.

So until my next, I am,

Always,

Your boy.

The Dilating Pupil

LAURA J. HIRD

HE HATED DRUNKEN teenage parties – even when he'd been a teenager himself he'd hated them. It always elicited a strange mixture of envy and disgust as he watched the adolescent boys perform their juvenile mating rituals and inevitably he would leave feeling wounded, misanthropic and well past his dead-by date. It wasn't so bad in class where he had some semblance of authority (on a good day) but he found the whole business of having to relate to pupils socially both demeaning and incredibly unnerving. When Jenny Russell had fixed him with that beguiling stare and asked him to her 16th birthday party, however, he'd simply been unable to say no.

Jenny's parents were on holiday so she'd told him to prepare for an uninhibited evening. Though he intensely disliked uninhibited adolescent boys – they were prone to violence and nausea – he wouldn't stay long. When the exam results came through, he had intended to take her to the theatre by which time she'd no longer be his pupil. They would see what happened after that.

He'd never really lusted after girls that young until he'd become a teacher. Of course, he didn't like them too young. Not like Mackay, the Deputy Head, who thought they were past-it by the time they reached their teens. There'd been a stunned silence in the common room when Mackay, fou, had blurted that one out at the Xmas party last year. However, he imagined this was more through its nearness to the bone than any sense of moral indignation.

You just had to hang about the pool when Stevenson was there with his boys. They all slagged Stevenson off because he was still single at 40, had a handlebar moustache and was devoted to the 5th form swimming team, but at least he wasn't blatant about it. The boys all seemed to like him. All the innuendo emanated from the younger, female staff who were worst of all. They were the ones who would rush in to watch Stevenson give swimming classes after school for what they called the 'crotch watch' – women in their thirties almost wetting themselves as the fourteen year old they called Paul 'The Pole' Dalzeil came out the changing rooms. But these same women had forced Alan Spencer to hand in his notice after a pupil had made allegations against him. It was rubbish as well, all in the girl's head. She had lived this fantasy that she was having a relationship with the guy but it was bullshit. Poor bastard! They caused such a hoo-hah about it he'd resigned out of embarrassment although everyone admitted privately it was all bollocks. It appeared to be fashionable amongst the female staff to accuse male teachers of lusting after jail-bait but the truth of the matter was they simply resented the competition.

He polished off a bottle of Claret with his dinner then rushed down several large whiskies in a pub near Jenny's house to brace himself. Suitably placated, he bought a half bottle from the local Pakis to see him through the next hour or so.

Entering her street, he checked the number on a postcard she'd scribbled the address on for him with the word 'PLEASE' underlined in large letters underneath. As he walked towards her house he contemplated just turning back but in his boozy sense of goodwill didn't want to disappoint her. He dutifully rung the bell.

She invited him in with a huge smile, looking stunning with a little eye make-up and scarlet lipstick accentuating her already full lips. Looking from her eyes into the hallway he edged past her.

'Sounds quiet. Many folk here yet?'

The room he followed her upstairs to he somehow expected to be full of pupils having a seance. It was, however, empty except for himself and Jenny. He smiled at her, not quite getting the joke.

'Am I too early?'

She looked slightly worried.

'Oh, don't be angry. I didn't actually invite anyone else.'

He continued smiling, awaiting elaboration. Turning her back to him she began putting ice into glasses.

'Have a drink. I just want to talk to you . . . on your own.'

Fumbling in his pocket for the half bottle he handed it to her.

'Here, don't drink your mum and dad's.'

Pouring two huge tumblerfuls she ushered him over to a lumpy armchair opposite the sink.

'Are you sure this is OK?'

'They're not back till Sunday. David's been staying at his girlfriend's.'

David was her brother. He'd taught him four years before but he was the bad and ugly to his sister's good.

Sitting on the floor cross-legged in front of him she sipped her whisky as he glanced around the room. It was her bedroom. A word processor on a desk by the window sat next to a pile of papers that begged to be asked about. Posters advertising art exhibitions, fringe shows and music festivals covered the walls. The Sylvia Plath, Jack Kerouac and Nancy Friday brigade lay proudly displayed on the top shelf of the bookcase, art and academic books in the middle, degenerating into Jilly Cooper and astrology self-consciously obscured by a straw waste paper bin at the base. The large single bed was covered by an emerald green paisley print duvet. He had a brief vision of her lying naked on it, exploring herself. He took a slug of whisky and smiled at her.

'Did you fall for any of the teachers when you were at school?'

He took another dram to recover from her forwardness.

'All the time.'

'Really!'

'Oh, I still do. Doesn't everyone?'

'What, you still have things about them?'

'No, I mean it just happens when you spend a lot of time with people in places you'd rather not be . . .'

She looked puzzled.

'. . . y'know – work, school – both if you're unfortunate enough to teach. A survival mechanism if you like. A nice wee infatuation now and again gives you an incentive to put up with all the bullshit and carry on.'

Uh oh. He was being too cynical. Or was he? She certainly looked very impressed.

'I sort of see what you mean. A bit depressing though, is it not?'

'Not as depressing as just going through the motions. Anyway, they're just harmless delusions to inspire me to do my job properly.'

Watching her sitting deep in thought, he realised what a lying bastard he was. He hadn't been able to do his job properly since he'd started teaching her. The rest of the class he treated like irritating obstacles in the course of his lust. Her work seemed standards above the rest of them but he wasn't sure how objective he was managing to be any more. Did it just seem that way because he read depth into any passage that translated in the direction of his ego?

'Don't you like teaching?'

'Not particularly. It's just something I ended up doing with my mediocre degree. Bear that in mind when you're faffing through college next year.'

'What about the pupils?'

'What about them?'

'Don't you like them?'

'I dunno . . . it's nothing personal . . . they just aren't really my favourite branch of the species, y'know.'

'That's some admission!'

'Ocht no, y'know . . . maybe the occasional one like yourself. Individually it's not so bad but large numbers of the buggers – nah – that's why I get paid for it. Anyway, I'm getting out of it soon. I might go back to Paris and work in a bar again – far less hassle!'

God, how long had he been kidding himself with that one – five, six years now. He hated Edinburgh – hated the way that before long everybody became a friend of a friend of a friend. It was so fucking incestuous, no wonder AIDS had spread so quickly. But the truth about teaching was that it seemed impossible to get out of it once you were in it. It usually took something drastic and even then there was only a temporary reprieve until he inevitably ended back in some shitty job in some shitty school or another – perhaps he'd become institutionalised. He finished his whisky. Taking the glass from him she poured another huge one.

'And what do you think of me . . .', she said with her back to him, '. . . not as a pupil . . . as a person, or a woman, whatever?'

As she handed him the drink, he felt her eyes scrutinising him.

'Well, I don't know, I . . .'

'Do you find me attractive at all?'

'Well, yes . . . you're very beautiful. You're always being told that though, you don't have to ask me.'

'Beautiful though . . . not sexy?'

He laughed to himself, pleased that she was trying to seduce rather than psychoanalyse him.

'Do you find me sexy?' she persisted, impatient for a compliment.

'I'm beginning to think you're an egomaniac.'

It was going to finally happen tonight. The air was awash with discarded caution. She seemed content to do all the running which suited him as he didn't want it to seem like he'd taken advantage of her. Some chance, the pushy cow.

'So you don't find me sexy? I'm not exciting you at all?'

'I'm absolutely underwhelmed!'

She stood up and smiled at him.

'Stop it. Stop being horrible.'

'Are we having a tantrum?'

'No.'

'. . . because I won't say you're sexy?'

She was embarrassed now. He was behaving like a teacher.

'Will I put some music on?'

'I don't know. Will you!'

'Stop it, I'm telling you.'

She put on some Aaron Copland. He listened to the first few bars before realising what it was. He remembered a conversation they'd had about that Copland piece at a bus stop last winter. As he finished his whisky his eyes scanned the room for the half bottle. It lay empty on her desk. She traced his gaze and stood up.

'It's all right if we drink a bottle of mum's. She's expecting it. She'll just be grateful I haven't wrecked the place.'

He didn't argue but told her he'd replace anything they drank the following day. Bringing an ice bucket and bottle of Grouse through from the kitchen, she filled his glass and sat down at his feet again.

'You're not married, are you?'

Had it never crossed her mind before?

'Divorced.'

'Will you tell me about it?'

'Tell you what? It's the usual story. Boy meets girl, girl turns into complete ball-buster, boy loses girl.'

'Do you still see her?'

'God, no . . . well, only very occasionally.'

'Do you still have sex with her?'

'And why would you want to know?'

'Just curious.'

He chuckled.

'No, we don't. Happy now?'

They did of course. Didn't all divorced couples? When they were at a loose end or between lovers. Not through any desire any more, of course. Just for a familiar, no-strings fuck.

'You're not planning on doing an Alan Spencer on me are you?' he sneered.

'I'm not a child,' she pouted.

He smiled and stroked her cheek because she was.

She replenished their glasses. He was feeling pleasantly

pissed and in control. Just as long as he kept one step ahead of her.

'Any more excruciatingly personal questions you feel you must ask me?'

She looked into his eyes.

'Will you kiss me?'

'Do you want me to?'

'What do you think?'

'Are you going to accuse me of date rape in the morning?'

'Why, are you going to rape me?'

'Not if you don't want me to.'

Laying her glass on the carpet she shuffled closer to him, relieving him of his drink and leaning against his legs. He kissed her lightly on the nose then sat back in the chair, laughing.

'Will that do?'

'I thought you were going to date rape me?'

'I'm still your teacher.'

'I won't tell anyone.'

'We'll take it slowly and see, will we?'

Her eyes flashed at him.

'Just one proper kiss and then we'll walk and *take it slowly*,' she mimicked.

'Just one then. We're still just friends though.'

He planted a few small kisses on her petulant bottom lip. She grabbed the back of his head, responding, trying to get her tongue in on the act. He pulled away and smiled.

'That wasn't very platonic now, was it?'

She blushed at him, her lipstick slightly smudged. Recovering his drink, he drained it and handed her the glass for replenishing. The whiskies she poured were huge. He liked women who poured sensible measures. They learned so young these days.

She handed him the glass then brought over a tin from the dresser.

'I know how I'll loosen your inhibitions.'

Prising open the lid she shook a large bag of grass in front of him.

'. . . since we're not telling anyone else about this anyway.'

He leaned over to have a look.

'Whose is that?'

'David's. He doesn't mind me using it though.'

'I'm sure he doesn't!'

'It helps with my painting. It inspires me . . . honestly . . . so he lets me use it.'

He imagined her brother being part of a drugs cartel. A gang of Jamaicans high on crack chasing him down the street.

'No, seriously Jenny. I don't think you should use it if it's David's.'

She unravelled the knot at the top of the bag.

'I do it all the time. He doesn't mind. He grows his own.'

He wasn't convinced.

'Won't your mother smell it when she gets back?'

'She's not back for two days. Anyway, she doesn't mind, she smokes it herself.'

He watched her sticking Rizlas together as he guzzled his whisky.

'Do you like grass?' she asked.

'I tried cannabis, you know the resin stuff, years ago. It didn't really do anything though, just made me laugh. This is my major vice.'

Gesturing to his whisky, he took a long drink and kissed the glass.

'I thought everyone smoked it.'

'Apparently not.'

'Apparently not,' she mimicked, laughing. Was his speech becoming slurred? The grass would calm him down.

Crawling across the carpet, she rummaged in a bag by the door and cursed to herself.

'I forgot to get cigarettes.'

'You don't need tobacco with grass, do you? Surely it's better without. It would ruin it.'

'I thought you'd never smoked it.'

'It's common knowledge Jenny, is it not?'

He hadn't meant to patronise her but if she was going to make him smoke the stuff anyway he wanted to make sure he felt something this time.

Standing up, she poured him another huge whisky then walked over to the CD player and changed the disc. The Doors.

'Is this OK?'

'I was a bit before their time I think.'

'You're not that old.'

He was hoping she'd say that. The tune was vaguely familiar though he wasn't really a great fan of that kind of music. Weren't they the band whose lead singer used to wank on stage? It sounded like he was singing, 'Show me the way to the next little girl.'

As she rolled the joint she asked him if he'd watched *Some Like It Hot* on television the night before. It was her favourite film. When he told her he'd gone to see it when it first came out she looked aghast.

'When was that? It was years ago, wasn't it?'

'No, 1960, 1959, something like that.'

She lit the joint and inhaled deeply.

'Don't worry, I'm not going to ask how old you are.'

'That's very decent of you.'

'Methuselah,' she whispered.

'You didn't seem too perturbed about my old age a few minutes ago.'

Ignoring his statement, she stood up, replaced the Doors CD with *Carmen* and took several large tokes on the joint until rich scented smog gushed from her nose and lips. This music sounded much better. Handing the joint to him she watched as he performed a ten-second session of staccato sucks then stared at her with a lockjaw grin as he held it in his lungs. Whooooooh! He felt it immediately. It felt wonderful, like a blanket of calm. Smiling normally now, he felt impressed with himself for not having had a coughing fit. A large gulp of whisky heightened his sense of machismo, then he repeated the process and handed the joint back to her. Taking a deep drag on it she fell into a daydream, jaw slightly ajar.

'That's the first time I've smoked in eight years,' he said, consciously trying to keep his voice deep.

Her pupils fixed on him and she looked tantalisingly raddled but didn't seem to register that he'd spoken. He tried again.

'I used to smoke fifty fags a day, then I stopped. Just like that . . .'

Clicking his fingers to emphasise the point, they made no sound.

'. . . plus, I learned a very important lesson in self-control when I stopped smoking.'

'And what was that?' she asked, seeming to pull herself together and edging across the carpet towards him, sleepily.

'What was what?'

'This important lesson in self-control?'

Oh yes, self-control. What had he being saying about self-control? He didn't have a clue so he listened to the music. It sounded even better now. Humming along, he tapped his glass in accompaniment. She looked up at him, bemused.

'I take it you like *Carmen* then?'

It made him realise he'd been singing out loud but despite his embarrassment he managed to summon scorn from somewhere.

'Oh, you know. It's terribly hackneyed nowadays. It's almost too embarrassing to listen to.'

'Shall I put it off?'

It really did sound good.

'No, don't worry about it.'

Relaxing again she leaned her arm on his leg. He watched her take a few sips of water. Water?

'What happened to your drink?'

She pressed the glass down on his thigh and traced the rim with her finger until it began wailing.

'I don't drink that much. I prefer smoking. It makes me feel sexy.'

His resistance to imminent seduction had greatly decreased. Why was he resisting anyway? He couldn't recall but it annoyed him that she thought she was taking advantage of him. What had they been talking about before? It was something safe he was sure. Oh yes!

'So what's your favourite bit in *Some Like It Hot* then?'

What an absolutely and utterly bloody boring question. No wonder she looked distant. She obliged him with an answer regardless and they began reciting their favourite lines from the film. She probably would have laughed at anything but he imagined she found him hilarious and was subsequently encouraged to go on and on and on . . .

'. . . and that bit where Jack Lemmon's in bed in the train and all the women climb up there for a party. You know, "*Watch that corkscrew!*"'

He knew he sounded nothing like Jack Lemmon, in fact he was speaking in a glaikit West Coast accent for no apparent reason but it seemed absolutely hilarious. He couldn't stop. The inane comments started coming thick and fast, punctuated only by his uninhibited snorts of laughter.

'Haw haw . . . noiboidy toakes lak thet. Haw haw Tony Curtis doing Cary Grant, did you realise, haw haw haw . . . know the bit I mean . . . noiboidy toakes lak thet . . . haw haw haw.'

Oh my God! What was happening? He was losing it. She laughed embarrassedly along with him at first but then began to look a bit bored. In an attempt to curb his bizarre outbursts he sucked extravagantly on the joint as she proceeded to roll another, then glugged down a mouthful of the whisky. It tasted fucking marvellous. The music whirled around his head as he watched her carefully cocoon more grass in a mosaic of cigarette papers. He kept going off on little gouches but another hit of Grouse soon perked him up. He stared at her until she looked back.

'What's this we're listening to now?'

She screwed-up her face in non-comprehension.

He elaborated. 'This music. It's fantastic. What is it?'

Still she didn't quite comprehend.

'*Carmen.* Are you joking?'

'Naturally,' he said, thinking he'd never heard the music before but it sounded wonderful. As she handed him the unlit joint she threw him another puzzled look.

'Here, I think you better spark this one up.'

Lighting it, he sucked at it greedily, interspersed with little sips of whisky until his head was spinning. As he got lost in the familiarity of the music she re-filled his glass. Oh yes, here it was. This was a good bit.

'Big boy, remembah, you must re-meeem-beerr . . .', wey hey! '. . . stand up and fight until you hear the bell, stand toe to toe, trade blow for blow . . .' off he went, more Terry Wogan's 'Floral Dance' than Paul Robeson.

'. . . keep punchin' till you make dem punches tell . . .'

Christ, he really could sing loud and his voice sounded brilliant. Really deep. Really powerful.

'. . . show that crowd what you know . . .', he serenaded, expecting her to look impressed, however, as soon as she sensed his glance she beckoned for the joint. Had he been hogging it? What the hell. She probably smoked it every day.

'. . . until you hear that bell . . .', he conducted himself, gesticulating wildly, trying to get her to join in, '. . . that final bell . . .' Despite her look of displeasure, this was the best bit so he sang it, inexplicably, in a shrill falsetto voice, screaming the final word, '. . . stand up and fight like heeeeellll!.' The singer finished a second or two after him. The CD was in Spanish or Italian, however, he preferred the American version about the boxer.

Oh shite! The look of alarm on her face suggested to him that he may have gone beyond the beyond. Grass really wasn't his scene. It made him feel wonderfully relaxed but this was counteracted by the knowledge that his sense of coolness and control were way out the window. It wasn't the drink. A fair skinful had been consumed but he could handle that. He'd been handling that for the past 25 years.

'You've never considered teaching music then?' she sniggered.

Reaching over impulsively, he took her hand and pulled her towards him.

'You're leading me astray, Jenny, I'm not used to this Bohemian lifestyle, you know.'

Kneeling in front of him she stroked his hand as he let his gaze run over her eyes, her lips, her small, tight breasts, her eyes, her lips and back to her eyes, watching her warm to him again, remembering why she'd invited him in the first place. The same thing worked in class. Twenty-nine pupils with their noses in books and the two of them in the midst of it, sitting across from each other, doing this – this visual intercourse.

Her fingers travelled, ever so gently, up and down his thigh. God, she worshipped him. It was so obvious.

'You should stop that, Jenny. I'll forget myself and do something unprofessional.'

But she merely did the same thing with his other thigh, gesturing to the floor with her eyes, luring him, inviting him.

Moving across the carpet she lay on her side with her head cupped in her hand. Adopting the same position he lay opposite, looking from her eyes to her lips to her eyes to her lips. As her mouth opened she let out a sharp, hot breath against his cheek. Pulling her head gently towards him, he watched her close her eyes and wait for his kiss, remaining like this, his face barely an inch from hers until she looked again to see the reason for the delay.

'What do you want me to do to you Jenny Russell?'

'Anything . . .' she gasped. '. . . everything!'

His fingers traced the outline of her thighs, hips, waist and down again. With each upwards motion he pushed the tight, little t-shirt she was wearing further up her body until her belly and the seam of her bra were exposed. Her lips were red and full and trembling, unlike his cock which, despite his arousal, didn't seem to be reacting at all. Listening to her breathing get heavier he watched her nipples strain through the white cotton, letting his fingers brush under them, feeling their fullness and heat as he continued his action up and down her body. She put her

THE DILATING PUPIL   149

mouth to his neck and moaned her warm breath against his shoulder as his hand slowly circled her breast.

'Do you like that?'

'Yessss.'

Lying back he pulled her on top of him. Coins spilt from his pocket and clattered onto the polished, timber floor. His cock was still not interested. Her tongue found his mouth and began examining his teeth and circling his tongue. As he rubbed his hands up and down her back more loose change spilt from his pocket. Her tongue was out of control, pushing into his mouth. It felt as if he was kissing Medusa and as he combed his fingers through her hair he imagined serpents rising to his touch. Her tongue was almost choking him. No, no. In an attempt to stop her probing he shut his mouth. Still no activity downstairs. Her tongue tried to break the barricade of his tightly closed lips. No, no, no. More coins drummed onto the floor. Fuck! He pushed her off him and sat up, flustered.

'Sorry, I'm like a fucking fruit machine here. Hang on.'

He emptied what was left in his trouser pockets into his jacket with the few coins he'd salvaged from the floor. A perfect vision of youth waiting to be defiled waited on the floor below. Lying on top of her with a worried determination about his soft prick, he kissed her smooth, baby-skinned belly, violently squeezing her firm, new, rounded breasts, muttering obscenities, trying to entice his prick to react, avoiding that off-puttingly inquisitive tongue. God, she was a terrible kisser. As he pushed her bra up her beautiful little, firm, new, rounded tits jumped out, begging to be sucked, fucked, fucking little bitch. Rubbing himself against her thigh – fuck, oh fuck, oh fuck what was wrong with him. Thinking of the ugly women and fat women and dirty women and old women he'd given the rides of their lives to in his time. Thinking of the red, varicose baby's arms they'd given him. He bit and sucked and kissed and nibbled and licked and imagined her sucking him off and imagined himself shooting all over her face and hair and sucked and bit and squeezed as she growled and squealed and pleaded for it. His mind grasped at favourite bits in porn films with women being taught how to suck cock and shagging two women as they lay on top of each other and their double pussies and fucking women's arses as they stabbed their cunts with dildoes. Jenny was grasping for his balls. He pushed her hand away. And women and men, women and women, women and lots of men, men and lots of women, men and girls, girls and girls, girls and horses, plump housewives in latex boots with spiky heels. Again she made a grab for his prick. Feeling a slight twitch, he ground against her hip bone to sustain momentum. Heavily made-up women with leaky mascara, women with mammaries the size of overladen shopping bags. Again, again, oh fuck, it was working. It was alright. Thank you God, oh yes, oh yes, he was going to hump the shit out of her. Dirty, filthy films with lurid names – imprisoned in silk panties and spanked to orgasm, all orifices filled, bend me over and choose your hole, strict aunties licking naughty nieces, girls sucking flashers, spank me harder and shag me. Fuck, fuck, fuck, fuck . . .

BZZZZZZZZZZZZ

'Wha . . . ?'

'Ignore it!' He continued thrusting against her but despite trying to respond her body had tightened up.

BZZZZZZ BZZZZZZZZ

Pushing him away she held her head up, listening, as if the sound wasn't loud enough.

'Ignore it. They'll go away.'

BZZZZZZZZ BZZZZZZZZZZ BZZZZZZZZZZZZZ

Pulling herself free she sat up on the floor.

'Shouldn't I answer it? I don't know who it is.'

'DON'T!' he yelled, trembling, annoyed and sounding exactly like a school teacher.

BZZZZZZZ BZZZZZZZ BOAZZZZZZ, nipped his brain.

'It must be important. Maybe something's happened.' She got up and stood by the door, desperate to answer it but scared of his reaction if she did.

'I don't believe this. I don't fucking believe this. I thought you hadn't invited anyone else.'

'I didn't. Honest.'

BZZZZZZZ BZZZZZZZ BOAZZZZZZZZZ

As he held his head and shrieked, his cock shrivelled away again. She stood fidgeting at the room door like a pupil waiting for permission to go to the toilet. Though devoid of any wish to have to entertain anyone else the idea was slightly more appealing than having her fish around in his cords and discover his deflated piece of loose flesh. After all that fucking struggle.

BZZZZZZ BZZZZZZZZ BOAZZZZZZZZZ

They looked at each other, distanced, waiting for the inevitable next . . .

BZZZZZZZ BZZZZZZZ BOAZZZZZZZZZ

'Answer it then! Go on!' he ordered, as if she'd been disobeying him by not doing so.

BZZZZZZZZ BZZZZZZZ BOAZZZZZZZZ

'. . . before I pull the fucking thing off the wall,' he muttered but she was half-way down the stairs before he finished talking. Tidying himself up he leaned back against the bed feeling wretched and impotent again. The sound of the front door being unbolted was followed by a young, male voice, then two people coming upstairs.

'Honestly, Jonah, I don't know where the key is. He'll have taken it with him.'

With part of her baby-skin belly still exposed, Jenny re-entered the bedroom with a half caste Asian youth he recognised from one of his previous fourth year classes. Shit. As the recognition dawned on Jonah an idiot grin wriggled across his face, his eyes darting around in their sockets like James Galway's.

'Exams coming up, are they?'

Jenny looked naïvely impressed at his sudden concern.

'Yeah, just three weeks now. Bummer, eh?'

Jonah threw back his head, roaring in amusement, then squinted down at him.

'Aaaaw, that must be how I failed them all. I thought I was just stupid. Pity they hadnae had swimming exams, eh?' he winked.

While he was contemplating a response they both left the room again. There seemed little point in an elaborate denial as that little shit wouldn't believe anything he said. He merely sat, dazed, watching and listening to them out in the hall. Jonah was trying to get into the room opposite Jenny's.

'Awe, come on Jen. Give's the key. C'mon. Dave said I could. Don't let's play silly wee lassies, eh.'

Jenny was gripping onto the doorknob, blocking him with her back.

'Come on. Stop fucking about. He's not harvested it yet. I know he's not. Gimme the key!'

They struggled with each other until the door eventually flew open.

Jenny crucified herself across the frame in weak obstruction but he pinched her hard between the legs, barging his way in when her body subsided in defence.

She came back through to the bedroom, shouting in a whisper.

'Tell him to stop. Get him out. He can't go in the attic. David'll go apeshit!'

Fussing and trembling and near to tears she stuffed the bag of grass down the front of her trousers, waiting for him to do something gallant.

'Look, it's none of my business, Jenny. I can't get involved. I shouldn't even be here.'

'Oh, thanks a lot,' she whined, going back into the hall, casting a hopeless glance into David's room and running back down the stairs. Jonah was pulling books out of the bookshelf and looking behind them, letting out little moans each time his search proved unsuccessful like the kind women make when they see seal pups on TV.

Leaving Jonah to his quest he escaped into the beckoning bathroom at the top of the hall. As he peed he heard her coming back upstairs and the argument resuming. Glowering at his flaccid prick, he hid it back in his trousers and considered just going home. He was on a high low from the grass and whisky and sexual struggles, however, there was also the now-or-never question to ponder. The thought of taking her out after the exams was rapidly losing its appeal. It would be too complicated, too much hassle. Of course he still wanted to fuck her, yes, but this preliminary crap took too much effort and made him feel ancient. Foreplay was bad enough but this – Jesus! And that grass had fucked him up too. He'd never have guessed that Jenny would be into all that, and who's to say it stopped there? She could be into anything. Fumbling in his shirt pocket he caressed the condom wrapper for reassurance. Sod it. Just brass it out for a little longer, fuck her and be done with it.

She was waiting, sheepishly for him in the bedroom when he got back through. Jonah was still rummaging around in David's room.

'I'm sorry I lost my temper a bit there. It's his fault. I had it all planned and he's spoiling everything.'

Mmm, 'planned'? Planning to seduce your teacher surely involved masturbation. Is that what she meant, he wondered. He purred inwardly.

'Anyway, he's just after a smoke,' she continued, shaking an envelope in front of him, 'He'll stay for one joint and then go.'

'You really think so?'

'Definitely, it's all he's after. I'm really sorry about all this. I'll make it up to you when he's gone.'

The enticing offer subdued his irritation somewhat but his nerves were still shot to bits. Jenny laid the envelope on top of her bookcase and went through to bring the glad tidings to the twitchy one. He came rushing back through behind her.

'Where? Where?' he screamed, his eyes devouring the room. No sooner had she pointed it out to him than he had it opened and was taking a flamboyant sniff.

'Oh ya beauty, ya fucking wee beauty!' he screamed at Jenny, humbled and happy at last. The idea that a toaty wee pile of smelly twigs could bring such jubilation in these materialistic times was slightly heartening.

'Can I skin up here, like. PURLEEEASE. I'm fucking gimping?'

His excited reaction was making her smile.

'Don't get too settled then. We're going soon.'

'Anything you say sweetheart. Anything you say,' however, he'd probably have agreed to anything since he was practically pishing himself with joy.

Jonah ran his fingers and wobbly eyes across the spines of Jenny's Penguin Classics, pulled out *Mrs Dalloway* and threw himself onto the bed, rolling a lethal-looking brute of a joint on it in the time it might take someone not travelling at cartoon speed to take the wrapper off a new packet of cigarettes and get one in their mouth. His joints were parsnips to Jenny's gentle runner beans. He found himself strangely captivated as Jonah gibbered on about Morocco trying to get into the EC and the European Commission telling them they had to clean up their act first, and his heinous tales of evil American drug enforcement people going over and spraying poison on all the cannabis crops. Tears welled in his eyes as this dreadful tale of man's inhumanity to man was emotionally recounted. What lives other people had to lead.

'Like it's serious shit, I'm telling you. No more solids, man. Plastic and diesel, that'll be it. The coffee shops in Amsterdam are even closing down, like, a few of them, I tell you. With the kikes getting stuck into the Lebanon again, like . . .' he nodded his head in despair. 'Its serious shit, I tell you.'

Shaking the envelope in front of them his face returned to its reassuring idiot grin.

'Fucking gold dust this, I'm telling you.'

He wondered if Jonah ended every sentence with the words, 'I tell you'.

Flamboyantly producing a zippo from the pocket of his denim shirt he lit the joint, taking in several lungfulls until his intense, jittery eyes shut and a sublime smile hatched on his mean little mouth. Reclining against Jenny's headboard he languished in it, savouring each draw like it was the final cigarette of a condemned man.

'Aw, that's beautiful, man. This is the longest I've gone without it for years.'

'How long has it been?' asked Jenny, enjoying the fact that she'd unwittingly brought light into someone's dark and dreary life.

'Three days, man. Three long fucking awful days. This famine's going to kill me, I tell you. I've fallen out with every cunt already.'

Edging over to the end of the bed, Jonah offered the joint to him.

'No, no thanks. I don't touch the stuff. Good job really by the sounds of it.'

Leaning over to get a better look at him, Jonah hissed through his teeth.

'Oh yeah! I'd see a doctor if I were you. Worst case of conjunctivitis I've seen in a long time.'

Shit. What was wrong with his eyes? He hadn't noticed them in the toilet, but then he'd been too busy lamenting his lifeless cock. He spoke, if only to change the subject.

'So what are you doing with yourself these days? Scrap metal business still doing well?'

Jonah looked confused. 'Eh?'

'Still liberating people's cars and crashing them I mean.'

'Aye, good one mate,' he smirked, rolling his eyes towards Jenny in a 'who-is-this-sad-fuck' way and handing her the joint.

'Not even the odd ram raid on bank holidays?' he continued, determined to undermine the little bastard.

Jonah shook his head and sat on the bed above him in an attempt to intimidate he supposed.

'Stealing motors is for neds, right. I'm a businessman now. Computer chip procurement consultant you might say. And I bet I make more than you do teaching, I tell you.'

Desperate as he was to give the little shit a right verbal

assault he recalled how easy to antagonise he'd been at school where he'd been expelled for belting a female teacher. Despite not wishing to find out if he still bore a grudge against the teaching profession, he couldn't resist a little dig.

'I always knew you'd make a success of your life.'

'Aye, fuck you!' Jonah whispered.

Jenny gave him a look of disgust and a sharp kick in the leg as she passed the joint back to her friend apologetically.

'Like I said. We've got to go out soon for this tutorial . . .'

Tutorial? What fucking tutorial?

'. . . so make one more for the road then we'll have to make a move.'

Jonah sucked at the joint from one hand, assembling cigarette papers and picking grass from the envelope with the other.

'So where's your "tutorial" then?' he drawled, mocking her use of a word so obviously alien to him.

'Oh, that pub in Dalry. What's it called again? The one opposite the garage?'

'The Balmoral?' they both yelped in disbelieving unison.

What was she raving about. Obviously she'd never been in the dive in question.

'So is it just the lassies get this treatment or is it some new concept in education?' he addressed him over the side of the bed. '. . . naw, naw, wait, don't tell me, it's the overcrowding?'

He resolved to try and humour the guy. Even the sharpest wit couldn't get one over on a numptie like him. You just spoke over their heads.

'It's just my way of making sure I'm not the only one going into school with a hangover in the morning, you know?'

'Ooooooh! Isn't he with-it?' minced Jonah, thrusting the

joint in front of him again, '. . . go on, surely a hip old thing like you can allow himself a couple of toaks.'

Upon his refusal, Jonah took two last puffs and ground the roach into the ashtray.

'So what time is this so-called "tutorial"?' he asked, lighting up the next joint before he'd finished exhaling the last one.

'About 10.30,' he interjected, thinking, it must be nearly that time, although he couldn't see the face of the alarm clock from where he was sitting. Jenny apparently could, however, as he noticed her cringing before Jonah looked up from his watch and chirped, 'Excellent. Plenty time to twist up a few more of these.'

The strong urge to just go home was again toyed with until the promise of that tight, young fanny made him decide to grin and bear it. Jonah now tore cigarette papers out of their packet, licking them together like a man possessed.

'I'll take a bit home with me too if you don't mind. Dave said I could, oh, and a glass of that Grouse would go down a treat.'

Jenny forced a tight smile, poured them all a drink and sat down in cross-legged resignation in front of them. Half an hour, two more whiskies and several joints were passed as they listened in virtual silence to Jonah giving a monologue about the evil of drink, the joys of drugs, security cameras, TV ads for football boots, the crime wave which would apparently follow the cannabis drought, a girl he thought fancied him who sounded more like she was on the verge of having him done for stalking, how over-rated *The X-Files* was, the dogs' dirt problem in Gorgie, what a slapper his father's new girlfriend was, Jimmy Corkhill in *Brookside* giving honest drug dealers a bad name, a boy called Dode he'd been at school with who used to make the young boys pee in front of him . . . My God he was a mine of useless information. With nothing but the whisky and the few puffs of a joint he'd had when Jonah was in the toilet to sustain him, he listened, fascinated, mute until finally, at 10.15, they left the house in a bid to finally be rid of this obnoxious, greedy paki.

The shock of the fresh night air after the stuffy claustrophobia of Jenny's room invigorated him briefly until the biting cold and space made him feel a bit weird. It had been foolish to take more of that grass but he'd needed something to see him through the bullshit he'd been forced to listen to for the past half hour.

Huddling his jacket round him for warmth and because it made him feel slightly safer he followed them down the street, consciously trying to walk as normally as possible, unable to remember what this entailed. As they reached the library the pungent smell of grass again invaded his nostrils and he realised to his horror that Jonah had lit another joint.

They stopped at the bus stop directly opposite a police caravan which had been set up as an incident room following the murder of a girl up the street the previous weekend. He kept a distance from them, happy in his assumption that Jonah seemed finally to be pissing-off but anxious about the possibility of surveillance from the police van.

Luckily, the only other person at the bus stop was a whisky-riddled old dodderer who, unable to negotiate which arm belonged in the sling around his neck seemed unlikely to notice the illegal aroma.

Pretending to be engrossed in the contents of the hairdressers window he watched them giggling round the joint in the glass. Surely if Prince Naseem buggered-off she wouldn't still expect them to go to that bloody awful pub? Jenny was dancing about on the pavement trying to keep warm, rambling on about the recent murder.

'Yeah, I'm sure I saw her on the bus the other week. She was English. It really looked like the girl in the paper. I don't think it was a serial killer or anything though. She was into drugs and that.'

Huh, she could talk! This area was the pits. He wanted the security of being back at her house. Forcing a few yawns to block out their being there he studied the reflection of the police caravan in the shop window. Jonah suddenly spoke really loudly and made him jump.

'Aye, she probably had the last piece of tarry in Edinburgh. I'd have cut her throat myself if I'd known,' he sniggered, presenting the joint to Jenny vertically to draw as much attention to himself as possible. It was as if he wanted to get caught. Maybe he did. Maybe that was the plan. What sort of a fucking wind-up was this? How long had they been standing there anyway? It felt like half an hour had passed.

Searching in his pockets for nothing in particular, just for something to do other than take them on, Jonah's loud voice echoed again,

'Fucking hell! This is a turn up for the books,' as a big, beautiful, blood-red, shiny number 34 twinkled ethereally round the corner of the brewery. He felt like kissing it. Unable to stop smiling he waited, knowing the moment of liberation was upon them.

As the bus opened its doors to rid them of this scourge, Jonah handed him the joint before disappearing on board, whooping with laughter. Throwing the offending article sparking into the air in an instantaneous reflex action he cursed as the bus pulled away taking the bastard, fucking little bastard, sneering from the window, with it.

Jittering, he turned to the old drunk, who was still utterly engrossed in his sling then to Jenny who was now, gloriously alone and grimacing.

'He does go on a bit. Sorry about that.'

Putting her arm in his she began leading him back along the street. He pulled away, teasing her.

'Hang on. Don't you want to go for that drink?'

Knowing he was joking she grabbed his hand and again pulled him towards the house, his cock giving an appreciative jolt as she did so. Staggering up the street together, hand-in-hand, they stopped to slobber over each other a few times before they reached the door.

Once back in the splendid safety of her house he pinned her against the anaglypta, crushing his lips against hers until she had to pull away for breath. He attacked her neck, biting, nuzzling, licking her ear-lobes, zip straining in a horny daze. No qualms now about her grabbing for his balls, he growled as she traced the outline of his stiff cock with her hand, gently biting her tongue as it again invaded his mouth.

Pushing her onto the stairs he chewed her nipples through the cotton t-shirt, yanking her jeans open with considerable, one-handed expertise. The remaining buzz from the stolen puffs of the joint took all the clumsiness out of their fondling. Intensified it. Made it all drift seamlessly into place like a fucking dream. Forcing his hand down her jeans he pushed his fingers under the flimsy wrapping of her knicker elastic, stroking her lusciously soft minge. Jesus, it was so soft. Did they just go wiry when they got into their twenties, he wondered?

'Not yet, not yet!' she gasped, wriggling under his touch.

Letting his middle finger press into the warm folds of her cunt he could feel her wetness, smell it. It seemed to swallow his finger in an envelope of moistness. She tried to pull his hand away, the epitome of 'stop-it-I-like-itness'. He continued ramming it in and out until he could hear her juices clicking.

'No, no, wait. Not yet. I want to make it better.'

Better? What could possibly be better than the sound shagging he was about to give her? Waggling free of him she zipped up her trousers and gestured to the bedroom.

'Come on. I've got a special treat for us first. To get us in the mood.'

In the mood? If he was any more in the mood his balls would explode. Dirty little bitch. Though aching to fuck her he let her draw it out to delay the inevitable disappointment when it was over.

The special treat was, unbelievably, a bottle of Moet her parents had given her for her birthday, which she messily cracked open over the rug. He'd for some reason been hoping that suspenders or handcuffs might be part of the special treat equation but pretended to be pleased none-the-less since he was now certain he was going to have her anyway.

The tin of grass made a reappearance and she sat at his heel showing him the flower-heads. Squeezing the oily, redolent herbs between his fingers he kissed the top of her head as she explained the difference between these and the leaves they'd been smoking earlier.

She rolled a joint as he sat in a dream, aware of something droning away in the background, imagining fucking her, what it would look like. Helping himself to more champagne he visualised his cock in her mouth, feeding his hard-on with filth, making sure it stayed where it was this time.

As she lit a much larger joint than her previous efforts, no doubt influenced by Jonah's monstrosities, he again checked his shirt pocket for the condom. There were more in his jacket if he needed them which, in his current state, seemed more than likely. He hated using the things but you really couldn't trust women nowadays. You didn't know where they'd been and now that single-parenthood was the fastest growing profession you had to be extra careful if you were a genetically-appealing specimen like himself.

Jenny put on some modern music of the all-beat and no melody variety, the kind that sounded like the noise blood made as it pumped round your body. Taking a few puffs on the joint and handing it to him she began dancing in front of him, thrusting her arms and hips in his face to the throb of the CD. Leaning his head back on the bed he watched her grinding away, Salome-like, through half-closed eyes and exhaled smoke. Gyrating over with the bottle she filled his glass, made him swallow it all down and topped it up again, twisting her lithe, tight young body as she did so.

The CD thumped on. It felt as if the sounds were emanating from within his rib cage. As a rule he despised this kind of modern crap but at the moment he could almost understand its appeal – its meditative, brain-clearing qualities. It was like when he went fishing and his thought and memory reduced to himself and the fish. Delighted with the analogy he wanted to tell her about it but found that he simply couldn't be bothered.

Standing with her feet between his legs she twisted, dreamily down until she was kneeling in front of him. With heavy eye-lids she took the joint from him, put the lit end in her mouth and blew smoke, through the roach, into his head. Wow, hey, he felt like he was floating, anaesthetized. Repeating the process she leaned back, laughing at his expression, whatever it might be, taking a slug from the bottle.

He squinted at her, drowsy, no longer feeling that he was

really there but that he was an observer, looking in. Fumbling around with a numb arm on the carpet at his side he found his glass and swallowed some champagne to liven himself up. The bubbles set off a series of tiny explosions at the back of his throat. Gulping back more of the grass to counteract this he again tried to explain what he'd been thinking about the music.

'You know these lamps you used to get in the seventies? Bowel-movement lamps?'

Jenny shook her head, clueless.

'Oh you know, these hideous bright orange things with kidneys floating up and down, passing each other, bits breaking off?'

'Are you tripping?' she asked '. . . it sometimes happens with this stuff.'

'No, no, no, no, no,' he whined, determined to make her understand, taking another puff to steady him.

'. . . no, no, it's like I was just thinking, this music, you know, sometimes when I'm out in the boat and its just, like, me and the fish, me and that fish for hours. Everything else just goes . . .'

Oh shit. His facility for coherence was away.

Seemingly frustrated by her own lack of understanding she blew more smoke into his mouth.

Oh dear, oh dear. Trying to deal with the ensuing weakness, powerlessness he tried to focus on the room, the sink, the bottle and glass at his side, Jenny sitting between his legs, puzzled, out-of-it, waiting for him to act. It was alright. It would be alright. He was safe here. He could stay here.

Jenny ruffled his hair, staring into his eye sockets, looking for him.

'Are you still in there?'

It was important to try and communicate with her, not to keep drifting off onto this strange parallel universe. Important to let himself know he really was still there and not just looking in.

'Erm, I think I'm starting to feel something . . . er . . . how are you? . . . how do you feel? . . . am I talking shit? . . . do you feel funny? . . . I feel a bit funny.'

She reminded him that the grass they were now smoking was different from the stuff she'd given Jonah. David charged more for the flower heads because they were a lot stronger. She didn't know why but he'd said they were well worth it. Worth it? The implications of her words made him panic. Perhaps it was mixed with something else. He hadn't felt like this when he'd smoked it earlier, that's for sure.

A creeping feeling of unease rubbed itself all over him, his stomach began rolling and he felt the blood draining from his head, then from the whole of his upper body to finally congeal in his legs. His legs! All sensation below the waist had gone. What if he needed the toilet? He'd better go for a piss now just in case.

On trying to stand up, the floor started moving, rocking from side to side like the inside of a galley on stormy seas. Holding onto the arm of the chair to stop himself from falling overboard, a voice echoed somewhere far off.

'What are you doing? Are you OK?'

His heartbeat began thumping in his ears. It was going too far too fast. Was he going to have a heart attack? This must be what it felt like. Where was he? He was going to have a fucking heart attack and he'd no idea where he was. Wanting to cry out he knew there was a reason that he couldn't though he'd no idea what it might be. Looking down in front of him he could see a road with lights on each side. There was a modern looking building with no windows and different coloured columns on top at the end of the street. The road reminded him of the Champs Elysées although he didn't recognise the building at the bottom. What the fuck was that building? Had they built a new Pompidou Centre at the bottom of the Champs Elysées? Why hadn't he heard about it? He'd had a strange dream that he was teaching in Edinburgh but he was still in fucking Paris.

The voice was echoing again. It sounded like someone was talking through a tube. 'Do you want any more of this? What are you doing?' It sounded like his mother but she was dead. He imagined his mother, naked, covered in ulcers with a great hairy fanny. Was it true? Did people come back to help you into the afterlife like all these psychic old women with names like Doris and Beryl had been saying for years? His heartbeat ticked through his head like some monstrous clock. He had to get to that building at the bottom of the street. He didn't know why, he just knew he had to get there. On trying to stand up he realised he was completely numb below the waist. Was it a brain tumour? Some kind of aneurysm? He had to get to that building. Now he was crying. He was still in Paris and he was crying and dying. Placing his hands on the support at his side, he pulled himself up with all his strength. The effort of the move made him fart loudly. He hoped there was no-one else in the street. He had a brief vision of someone lying on a bed at his feet, masturbating and laughing hysterically. Making his way towards the building, it felt like he was walking up the side of a mountain although the road ahead looked flat. Taking one step at a time, pausing between each to catch his breath, tears burnt his face. The voice was calling him again. 'Laissez moi seule, laissez moi seule,' he shouted. He sensed someone stomping away and heard a door slamming.

Although the building had looked like it was at least a mile away he made it there in six steps. Falling against it, his hands shot to each side of the roof to steady himself. The columns on top were painted to look like tins and bottles of brand-name toiletries. Fucking modern architecture. The roof itself had an empty swimming pool on it with two enormous carved taps at the side. Looking down as a fountain of sick sprayed from his trembling mouth, he tried stemming the flow with his hand but the vomit merely spurted through his fingers, down his chin and shirt. Four such ejaculations and the pool was half full. It reeked of whisky and garlic. Spaghetti floated about in the pottage like sea snakes.

He sensed that there was someone with him. Trying to remember where he was or what he'd been doing before he'd taken ill, he heaved again. There was an appalling pain in his stomach and he could feel his windpipe burning where the vomit had scorched it, but somehow throwing up made him feel slightly better, slightly calmer despite his conviction that he was dying. By now he was only bringing up acidy bile. The swimming pool looked like a swamp. He negotiated the taps at the side. Were they merely ornamental? He twisted one until a gentle piddle of water ran into the vomit sending off shock waves of yellow, greasy film on the surface of the plum-coloured broth.

Someone or something was touching him, trying to drag him away. Unable to form a sentence he merely groaned. The pool was now overflowing, his watery vomit running down the sides of the building. He was being led back the way he'd come. The lights on the side of the road had gone out and there were now swirling patterns surrounded by a dimly lit tunnel. He let the arms guide him and steady him each time he stumbled. Since he was dying anyway it no longer mattered if this was friend or foe. He felt himself being turned around and thumped in the chest. This was it. Like falling backwards in a dream then waking just before you made impact, but he had made impact and hadn't woken up. Now he felt strangely comfortable. Was it over? Was he dead? Closing his eyes, he basked in the silence, blowing out breath, blowing out life. He was slipping away now. He was probably lying in a hospital somewhere. The machine that monitored his heartbeat was about to go 'Eeeeeeeeeeeeeeeeeee'. His pulse was about to stop. A casualty nurse was about to sigh and say, 'The pupils have fixed. That's it.' He waited behind the darkened silence. Had someone been with him? Hadn't Jenny Russell been with him? No, he was still in Paris. There was no Jenny Russell. As he listened to his breath getting shorter and shorter, weaker and weaker, he blacked-out.

He came to on the armchair with a blanket over his head, delirious from the toxic fumes he'd been breathing in and out all night. His head throbbed from one temple to the other and he felt like he'd been pushed down a flight of stairs. His bladder was painfully full and an erection strained to be liberated from its corduroy captivity. Jenny was lying asleep on top of the bed by his side. Her knees were bent and her legs had fallen apart like a woman in stirrups waiting for a smear. Had he fucked her? The blanket over his head suggested not.

Finding the bathroom he gulped water from the tap then left it running while he masturbated unenthusiastically onto a few sheets of toilet paper, staring at his ravaged, bloodshot face and the large, purple love bite on his neck as the tension arched out of his cock. He threw the tissue into the pan and pissed onto it then washed the previous night's debris from his face and unblocked his caked eyelids. Breathing into the towel he squirmed with recollection then walked quietly back through to the bedroom.

The sink had been washed out but the carpet was still damp and the rank stench of his flamboyant failure hung in the air to taunt him. Jenny was snoring gently. Sunlight beamed through a chink in the curtains and spot-lit her soft pubic down and the glistening, wet indentation of her cunt. She'd slept that way deliberately he reckoned.

He knew he should probably wake her – apologise profusely, blame it all on a bizarre medical condition, fuck her into forgiveness then refuse to leave until he was convinced she'd keep quiet about the whole thing but the truth was he just couldn't face facing her. Couldn't bear the idea that this horribly confident little shit had seen him with his pants down in a sadly less than biblical sense. Again his mind was turned to Paris. That safe haven just the other side of revision periods and examinations, perhaps sooner. He cast a final glance upon her dignified indignity splayed on the bed, left a £20 note on the bedside table for the whisky, picked up his jacket and tiptoed downstairs.

As he opened the front door to let himself out he noticed Jonah sitting in his boxer shorts in the living room smoking a joint. This vision which cruelly reaffirmed that it had not all been a bad dream gave him a painful lump in the pit of his stomach. The sinewy Asian, noticing him, held up the joint and opened his mouth to speak, but before he had a chance to he ran out the house, slamming the door behind him. He kept running until he got to the end of her street then walked the rest of the way home in the blinding sunlight, despising her and her sort.

The Rosewell Incident

IRVINE WELSH

For Kenny, Craig and Woody

1

ANOTHER CONVOY OF travellers hustled along through
the busy traffic which clogged the city's arteries, rolling
onto the slip-road off the congested by-pass and snaking
painstakingly towards the mobbed field which rumbled with
the buzz of small competing sound systems.

From the disused railway bridge overhead, a sweating PC
Trevor Drysdale kept a watchful eye on the scene. Drawing a
wheezy breath of the baked, mucky air, Drysdale whipped his
brow and gazed heavenwards at ragged clouds which failed to
block out the sun's leery heat.

Out off the range of Drysdale's vision and earshot, in a
stinking enclave underneath the concrete by-pass, the local
young team were also filling their lungs with the chemicals
the traffic spewed out, to complement the ones they voluntarily
ingested.

Despite the heat, Jimmy Mulgrew felt himself shudder. It
was the bevvy and the drugs, he reasoned. It always kept a
part of you from being warm. That, and lack of sleep. He
embarked on another flinching spasm, more severe than the

last, as Clint Phillips, standing over a prostrate Semo, brought the heavy hammer crashing down on the side of the boy's strong, square, jaw. This jaw was concealed by the pillow Semo had wrapped around his head and secured with tape over his face, which left only his eyes and mouth visible. Even with this protection, Semo's head still jolted to the side under the impact of Clint's blow.

Jimmy looked across at Dunky Milne, who raised his brows and shook his shoulders. He took a step forward and wondered whether or not he should intervene. Semo was his best mate. But no, Clint was staying cool and checking on him. – Awright Semo? Is it away? Is that it broke, aye?

Semo looked up at Clint, registered his ugly smile. Even wasted on a Temazapam capsule and some superlager, Semo could still feel the pain in his jaw. He moved it around. It was sore, but still intact. – It isnae broke yit, he drawled, his spittle dribbling into the pillow.

Clint bristled, taking on a prize fighter's gait. He turned and shrugged to Jimmy and Dunks, who looked back neutrally at him. There was something moving uneasily in Jimmy's chest, and he wanted to say 'that's enough' but nothing came out as Clint crashed the hammer with viscious force, into the side of Semo's head.

On impact, Semo's head jerked again, but then the boy staggered to his feet. An old man walking a labrador dog looked startled as he turned the corner and came upon them. The young team's stares burned him and he pulled the pissing, whining beast along the road as it tried to urinate on one of the concrete support pillars. The man disappeared around the other bend that led up from the slip road to the old village, before he had the chance to witness the youth with the pillow taped around his head tear the hammer from the other boy's grasp and smash him full in his unprotected face with it.

– FUCKEN RADGE! Semo roared, as Clint's cheekbone shattered and part of his top row of teeth were scattered in a sickening splintering sound which fused Jimmy with a nauseous but uplifting feeling. Jimmy didn't really like Clint, basically because Clint worked in the garage and Shelley hung around there, but he also wasn't enthusiastic about this scam.

Clint was holding his face in his hands, looking up at Semo and screaming like a demented Hyena, spitting blood and teeth. He turned to Jimmy and Dunks in tearful appeal, – It wisnae meant tae be me! he bleated, – It wis meant tae be that cunt! He hud the fuckin jelly! He hud the pillay!

Semo looked completely away with it. He wasn't letting go of the hammer, nor was he removing his rapacious gaze from Clint.

– It's done now but, eh, Jimmy shouted. – Moan, lit's goan see the polis! He winked at Semo, who let the hammer rest by his side.

– Fuck youse! Clint whined, – ah'm gaun hame!

– Come back tae mines, Jimmy said.

Clint was in no position to refuse, allowing himself to be led back to Jimmy's house. They went upstairs to Jimmy's room, and listened to some tapes. Clint managed to swallow two jellies and passed out on Jimmy's floor. Jimmy went downstairs for a binliner and put it under Clint's head, to stop the blood from getting everywhere.

Jimmy started to relax when he heard his father turning up the volume on the telly's handset downstairs, so he increased the output from his Bass Generator tape. As the telly volume nudged up an increment, so Jimmy corresponded. It was a familiar ritual. He smiled at Dunky, and gave the thumbs up and they opened a tube of Airfix. Clint was out for the count, and Semo was also asleep. Jimmy tenderly cut the tape and let the pillow flap back and his friend's head rest naturally. Semo's jaw was badly swollen, but his injuries were minor in comparison to the mess Clint's coupon was in. Letting a couple of drops of the nippy, burning liquid drip onto his tongue, Jimmy felt himself satisfyingly struggle for breath as the vapour filled his lungs.

2

Shelley Thomson had six toes. When she was wee her father told her that she was an alien from outer space and that she was found abandoned by her parents when a UFO dumped her in a field outside Rosewell. The truth however, was that it was her father who had abandoned Shelley. When she was six years old, he simply did not come home one day from work. Her mother, Lillian, refused to tell Shelley whether she knew anything at all about her dad's disappearance.

As a result, Shelley somewhat idealised the memory of her father, and this was particularly the case in times of her adolescent battles with Lillian. Growing up into a dreamy, speculative fifteen year old, Shelley had developed a fascination for UFO's.

When she realised that she was pregnant after missing two periods and then scoring two positive tests on a Boots' home testing kit, Shelley claimed that the father was a seven-foot alien who came to her in the night and took her semi-conscious to a place which may or may not have been a spacecraft and lay on top of her. She told her friend Sarah that there was the 'feeling of doing it' without any genital interaction.

– Aw aye? Sarah scoffed, – what was eh like? Keanu Reeves? Liam Gallagher?

Sarah tried not to show that she was impressed that her friend did not allow herself that kind of indulgence. Instead Shelley described the alien in classical terms: a long, thin hairless body, large slanted eyes etc. Impressed though she was, Sarah was far from convinced.

– Aye, right Shelley, she disdained. – It's Alan Devlin's fae the garage, eh?

– Nuhp!

Alan Devlin was an attendant at the local garage at the bottom of the slip-road which led onto the by-pass. He had a charming manner with young girls from the local school, whose grounds backed onto the filling station. Clint Phillips, Alan's bashful seventeen year old YT would wait nervously outside and keep watch while the senior attendant indulged himself in the backshop with the local youngsters, Shelley and Sarah being amongst those whom he numbered in his schoolie harem. Clint longed for a piece of the action but was too shy in himself, due mainly to his bad spots, and therefore too unexotic to the girls, and Devlin would tease him mercilessly about it. Many times Clint wished that Mr Marshall, the garage manager, who was never there, would come by and surprise them, but he never did. Marshall was an alcoholic and always on the piss in one of the local pubs come lunchtime. Clint liked to infer that he'd fucked Shelley; this annoyed the fuck out off his mate Jimmy Mulgrew, who had the hots for her in a big way.

Alan Devlin came from the city and had been involved with a gang of football casuals known as the Capital City

Service in his teens, but gave up when his older brother Mikey mysteriously vanished one evening, never to return. Mikey Devlin had been a top boy and it had been five years since his disappearance. Alan Devlin's strengths with young girls were his charm and persistence. Shelley had allowed Alan to fuck her after hearing this story. As her father had vanished, she felt a bond to Devlin. Previously, this tall, thin schoolgirl had only let him touch her small, pubescent breasts, often as he and Sarah had full intercourse. Devlin had re-evaluated life since the vanishing of his big brother, whom he had idolised. The gig was basically fucked, you were here one minute and gone the next. The point was to take what you can get. For him, this meant shagging as many birds as possible.

Shelley, and for that matter Sarah, always vowed never to visit Alan in the garage again. They were invariably drawn out of boredom however, and unfailingly flattered by the older lad's easy charm. Before they knew it, Alan's hands would be all over one, or both, of them.

3

The shantytown of travellers had spilled from the old municipal travelling people's site, onto the toxic wasteland alongside it. The settlement was growing daily. Millennium fever: these wee cunts were crazy for it, thought PC Trevor Drysdale. They weren't real travelling people, they were just cheeky wee cunts out for bother. As if he didn't get enough of that from the local youths. There had been a fight outside the chipshop last night. Again. Drysdale knew who the troublemakers were, with their drugs and smart-arse behaviour. Later this week he was up before the promotion board. There was still time to get the kind of result that could swing it. Had he not scored brownie points with his firm, but sensitive dealings with the travellers? Sergeant Drysdale. It sounded good. That new suit from Moss Bros. It fitted like a glove. Cowan, the chairman of the promotion board was a sticker for appearances. Brother Cowan was also known to him from the craft. The job was as good as his.

Drysdale walked down the path to the edge of the reservoir. Beer cans, wine bottles, crisp packets, glue tubes. That was the problem with working-class youth today; economically excluded, politically disenfranchised and full of strange drugs. It was a bad combination. All these wee cunts wanted to do was to party into the next century and see what this cultural watershed brought. If the answer was 'the same old shite', as it surely would be, Drysdale morosely reflected, then the wee fuckers would just shrug and party on into the next one.

Trevor Drysdale knew that there had never been a golden age of the 'clip round the earhole' in enforcing the law in these parts. Yet he did remember the realpolitik equivalent of social control, 'the kicking in the cells'. The old school of rough and ready Scottish youth respected that great institution of law enforcement, the slippery steps. Now though, most of them were too full of drugs to feel the kicking or remember they'd been given it. After a few jellies, that kind of damage went with the territory. Yes, such an activity could still be therapeutic for the individual officer, but as a method of enforcing the law it was worse than useless.

What a place, Drysdale mused, letting his gaze sweep over the reservoir down across the city's topography and back up to the Pentland Hills. It had changed here alright.

Even as conditioned to its incremental development as he was, sometimes the nastiness of the arbitrary, incongruent nature of the place jarred him. Old villages, shoebox modern housing developments, barren fields, scabby farms, industrial estates, leisure and shopping complex's, motorways, slip roads and that rancid piece of brown, derelict wasteland they bizarrely called the Green Belt. That terminology seemed like yet just another calculated insult perpetuated on the locals by the authorities.

But if there was one thing that concerned him more than the gloom which had solidified the place like a gel, it was this new wave of optimism. Millennium fever. In other words another excuse for young cunts to go shagging and drugging while the rest of us have to work away in a state of loathing and fear, he considered with rancour, feeling his ulcer bite. It had to be stopped. There were thousands of them now, crowded onto that strip of land.

Drysdale looked down from the steep bank by the water. He could see that makeshift village of lost souls expanding, getting closer and closer to his own Barratt estate. Thank fuck for the sliproad that divided them. It was surely now time for the Government to declare a national emergency; take off the kid gloves. But no; the sly fuckers were holding off, crossing their fingers for a few drug-related deaths. Then whip up hysteria amongst a supposed moral majority and bring in some more repressive measures. It had to be worth a few percentage points in the polls, and party conference season, and an election itself, were coming up soon. There would be a round of 'get tough' speeches followed by a few witch-hunts. Drysdale had heard it all before, but to hear it more loudly would at least mean that they hadn't given up. Let's get some fucking blood spilt here, he ruefully willed, despatching a rusty can into the dank water with a crisp volley.

4

The young team's plan had been an inadvertent success. The next morning Clint Phillips woke up on Jimmy Mulgrew's floor in agony, and they had been forced to take him to the hospital, where he was x-rayed, detained and admitted. Jimmy considered it a bonus that Clint, rather than Semo had been hospitalised, although with Clint not at the garage shop, they would have to watch what they nicked with that big Alan Devlin cunt around.

Anyway, Clint would be out in a day or so, then they could go round to the small police sub-station, and register the crime with the polisman Drysdale, blaming a group of the travellers for the assault.

5

The Cyrastorian pushed his long fingers against his temples. He could feel himself steadily moving from the centre of The Will, out into the peripheral zones of its influence. Sometimes Gezra, The Elder, felt that he had been wrong to pursue this line of work beyond his allotted span. It was as if he could feel the very chill of deep space, insinuating itself into his flesh and bone, through the translucent aura of The Will, which protected him and all his world's sons and daughters.

In the darkness of his craft, illuminated only by the screen which panned up images of the observed planet, The Appropriate Behaviour Compliance Elder for this sector pondered as to likely destiny of the rogue youth's ship. Earth seemed almost too obvious. After all, their specimen had been from that world. Specimen, Gezra smiled across his thin lips, he would have to stop using such a pejorative, demeaning term. After all, the Earthman had been inducted, electing to stay a part of Cyrastorian culture, rather than return home with a memory wipe, and all in return for strangely modest rewards. There was little to be gained in attempting to understand the primitive psyche of the Earth creature.

The Appropriate Behaviour Compliance Elder reluctantly decided that he needed to use external technology to locate the renegade youths. This prospect filled the Elder with distaste. Cyrastorian philosophy was based around the dismantling and demobilising of external technology, and the ruthless promotion of The Will, those individual and collective psychic powers, by which his race had developed and advanced their civilisation from their own decrepit, post-industrial age, now several millenniums past.

As with Earth humanoids, the early history of Cyrastor had been dominated by a procession of prophets, evangelists, messiahs, sages and seers who had contrived to convince both themselves and their followers that they were privy to the secrets of the universe. Some achieved little more than ridicule in their own lifetime, others would have an influence on generations.

The remorseless rise of science and technology conspired to undermine the great religions as the basis of truth, without ever reducing the humility, wonder and reverence experienced by all intelligent life forms as they contemplated this immense, amazing universe. Yet as Cyrastorian technology itself advanced and opened up what seemed like a vast expanse but would retrospectively only be regarded as a corner of their civilisation, it simultaneously threw up more mysteries than it had the capacity to resolve. This was always the way with knowledge, but of greater concern to the Cyrastorians was their culture's inbuilt tendency to gear all such technology towards the consumption of resources without being able to eliminate poverty, inequality, disease and the wasted potential of its citizens.

At the very height of their technological advancement, this pragmatic and idealistic people faced up to their spiritual crisis. A body called The Foundation was established by Principal Elders. Its brief was to promote spiritual enlightenment, and to liberate the Cyrastorian potentialities of the mind from its hitherto supposed physiological limitations. Centuries of mediation resulted in the creation of The Will, a collective pool of psychic energy upon which every Cyrastorian could draw and, by the very act of living and thinking, contributed to in accordance with the levels of their personal training and their ability to learn. As The Will had all but eradicated cultural and social differences, this access proved to be very similar in all Cyrastorian citizens.

It had previously been somewhat hilarious for Gezra to fritter away leisure moments watching primitive cultures like Earth continue down their blind alley of external technology development. Now however, many of the renegade Cyrastorian youth were into this visceral touch, feel and taste nonsense. They were seeking physical types of interaction for its own thrilling sensation, and seeking it with races who were little more than savages. Gezra knew however, that the renegade leader, the Younger called Tazak, had, for all his rhetoric about the cult of physicality, extremely developed psychic powers, and would sense any Elder attempts at the detection of his presence through the exercise of The Will.

6

The young team were sitting drinking cheap wine by the reservoir. Jimmy remembered that, only a few years ago, they had fished for perch and pike in its waters. Glue had taken over. It wasn't really that it was less boring, more that being glued up was like the excitement of a catch spread over the whole day. There was an aroused sense of wasted purpose and at the same time a comfort in the oblivion it produced. Of course, they all knew that it was going nowhere. While intoxication provided a multitude of misadventures, tales of which could, under certain conditions, get you through periods of mind-crushing straightness, it too often only led to greater frustration and anxiety.

But fuck it though, Jimmy yawned and stretched, feeling the pleasurable unravelling of his limbs, you always tended to follow the line of least resistance. What else was there? Jimmy thought of his parents, now split up, their quaint notions of 'respect', hued from an era of full employment and half-decent wages, floundering on the remorseless, depressive nothingness around them. He couldn't respect them, nor could he respect society. He couldn't even respect himself, only band together with his pals to enforce others to respect him, in a way which became more limited and proscribed every day. You just had to stick together with your mates, and make sure there was a clear tunnel ahead and hope for a better world if and when you emerged into the light.

The travellers maybe had the right idea, Jimmy thought. Perhaps movement was the key. Why the fuck had the sad cunts come here though? The stretches of wasteland, between the Barratt schemes, industrial estates and fly-overs, had become home to people from all over Britain and even further afield. All those fucked up cunts, talking about a 'force' that brought them here. Here! For fuck sakes. Anyway, to fuck with all those cunts, Clint was out tomorrow. They'd register the crime with Drysdale and then take the criminal compensation cunts to the cleaners. Easy.

Jimmy swigged back half a bottle of Hooch lemonade. They had graduated to beer and spirits, their current favourite tipple being a few Hooches, superlager and fortified wine with capsules of Temazapam if available. Their mate Carl had almost drowned the other week, falling asleep by the side of the reservoir, only for it to rise in the evening. When the others had staggered back into town had caught up with him, it was nearly over his mouth and nostrils.

Looking up at the ugly, hollow sky, Jimmy wondered if there was anything out there. This was one of the top places in Britain for UFO sightings and every six months or so, scientists and journalists and UFO spotters would be seen hanging about the town. It was always in shitey redneck places like this where there was fuck all to do that people saw those things, he reflected bitterly, lobbing an empty bottle into the reservoir. Why the fuck would aliens come here? He'd been talking to that dippit wee Shelley too much, her that was getting fucked by that Alan Devlin cunt, the city boy from the garage. He resented the city boy, not just for fucking a girl he had sexual designs on (after all he had sexual designs on almost any girl) but because Devlin had threatened to baseball bat him after he had caught Jimmy stealing some crisps.

It had to be said though, Shelley was pure class. Jimmy knew that from the time at the chippy when he had offered to buy her chips; she had asked for curry sauce on them. It was these wee touches that marked out the top manto from the park and ride brigade. But this aliens baws though, it got on his nerves. That was how that Alan Devlin was riding her, getting her head messed up with all that shite.

Glue had always been Jimmy's drug of choice. He loved the stunning rush of the vapour, the way it stuck to his lungs, catching his breath. He knew that it meant he possibly wouldn't live long, but as every auld cunt in the town was as miserable as fuck, so there seemed to him to be no real virtue in longevity. It was quality of life that counted and he considered that you were better being cunted than on a fuckin scheme for a pittance with some red-faced toss-bag shouting at you and then paying you off after two years to make way for the next dippit cunt. If any cunt couldn't see that, then, as far as Jimmy was concerned, they didn't have a fuckin brain. – The logic is inescapable, he sniggered to himself.

– What you sayin ya daft cunt? Semo laughed.

– Nowt, Jimmy smiled, dropping some Airfix model glue on his tongue, enjoying the nip and the sensation of asphyxiation. Then, when air filled his lungs, he savoured the spinning in his head. As the throbbing in his temples receded, he squirted the rest into an empty crisp packet and went for it.

– Pass it ower Jimmy ya cunt, Semo moaned, guzzling a can of superlager and wincing. It tasted foul. You were better starting on the Hooch until you got cunted enough no tae taste the lager, he decided. It wisnae too bad cauld, but warm . . . fuck it.

Jimmy reluctantly passed the bag to Semo. For a brief second he felt that the ground was going to rise up and smack him on the chin, but he weathered that storm and rubbed his eyes in an attempt to restore some vision.

Dunky was chewing on something or other. – Mind when we used tae fish here? Good times, he mused speculatively.

– Borin as fuck but, eh, Semo said, then with a sudden abruptness which caused Jimmy to start inside, – Hi, you rode that Shelley yit Jimmy? Yuv been sniffin roond it enough.

– Mibbee ah huv, mibbee ah huvnae, Jimmy smiled. In his fantasy they were going out together. He liked the way people were starting to associate them. He played his desire like a poker hand, flirting with his friends about his feelings for this girl, in a strangely deeper way than he actually did with her.

– Some cunt wis sayin she's up the kite, Dunky said.

– Fuck off, Jimmy snapped.

– Jist gaun by what ah fuckin heard, Dunky replied, unconcerned. He rolled over, feeling the blazing sun bite into his face.

– Dinnae fuckin spread aroond stories, right, Jimmy dug in. He knew it was that cunt Clint, with his big mouth. He could see Clint's huge, loose, slavering gob, just before Semo shut it so deliciously with that hammer. He could see Alan Devlin, shouting at him to put they fuckin crisps back. He could see, in his mind's eye, the smiles Devlin got from the girls, including Shelley, and how powerless they seemed to be to do anything but giggle with a sexy nervousness under his patter. Jimmy had tried Devlin's style, but it never hit the mark, not in the same way. He felt like a little girl secretly putting on her mother's dress.

– Aye, right, Dunky scoffed.

Dunky wasn't really making an issue of it, but Jimmy was. He stood up and jumped on top of his friend, pinning him to the ground. He grabbed a handful of Dunky's red hair and twisted. — Ah sais dinnae fuckin spread roond stories! Right!

In the background Jimmy could hear the encouraging wheeze of Semo's low, mirthless laugh. Jimmy and Semo, always Jimmy and Semo. Just like it was always Dunky and Clint. Semo's hammer had been symbolic, it had changed the balance of power between the four of them. This was in case Dunky forgot exactly what that blow had meant. — Ah sais right!? Jimmy growled.

— Right! Right! Dunky squealed as Jimmy relaxed his grip and rolled off him. — Fuckin radge, he moaned, dusting himself down.

Semo sniggered uncontrollably, — Ah'd ride her, he said. — Ah'd ride her mate n aw. That Sarah. That would be awright, eh Jimmy. You wi that Shelley n me wi that Sarah.

Jimmy allowed himself a smile. Semo was his best mate. The concept was not without appeal.

7

Shelley was reading *Smash Hits* while her mother was making the tea. Liam out of Oasis was a shag, she considered. Abby Ford and her pals at the school were always going on about Oasis. Abby Ford always seemed to have the money for clothes and records. That was why all the laddies at the school were hanging around her. Shelley had to concede that she liked the way Abby wore her hair. She would let hers grow. She'd been daft to get that crop, but it had annoyed her mother. Abby was okay, although Sarah didn't like her. Shelley and Abby had chatted a bit. Maybe her and Sarah would become pals with Abby Ford, Louise Moncur, Shona Robertson and that crowd. They were alright. Shelley wished that she could get the money for good clothes.

But Liam out of Oasis. Mmm hmm. Better even than Damon or Robbie or Jarvis. Looking deeply into Liam's eyes, in that picture Shelley fancied that she could see a bit of his soul in them. It was as if he was staring only at her. Shelley Thomson convulsed appreciatively that only she could crack this secret code in these eyes, and feel this bond between them. It would be great if Liam could meet her, possibly when Oasis played Loch Lomond. He would see what a great pair they would make, and that they were really meant to be together! Love at first sight! She didn't know whether she would keep the baby or get rid of it. That would of course be up to Liam as well; he would have to be consulted. It was only fair. Would he want to bring someone else's child up as his own, an alien as well? If he loved her, and she could tell, by the way he looked at her, that he truly did, then it would present no problem. It would be brilliant if Sarah married Noel. That would make them sisters-in-law. How good would that be?

– Shelley, tea, her mother said briskly. Shelley put down the copy of *Smash Hits* and went up to the table. The image of Liam's soulful, brooding eyes still burned and she imagined him touching her breast and felt a fluttering current of electricity in her stomach. She sat down to oven chips, sausages and beans, eating in brisk, economical movements. Shelley ate like a horse, and even though she was pregnant, (she didn't know for how long, having had very little morning sickness), she was as thin as a rake. She was crazy for chips, she loved the ones at the chippy, especially with the curry sauce. Her Ma's chips; small, crinkly and ungenerous, they never really cut it.

She was different from her mum, she smugly reflected. Her mother, who just needed only to look at a McCains oven chip for another few not-quite imperceptible fat cells to form. Shelley saw this as a defect in her mother's character. Her mother looked haggard. And bloated. Was it possible to look both at the same time? Too right, Shelley thought, looking up at Lillian staring out of the window from behind the net curtains, a fearful expression on her face. She always seemed to be thinking about something ominous. Shelley had to keep in with her though. Her mum liked Oasis as well. There was the possibility, slight, but nonetheless real, that they would go to Loch Lomond together. Her mum once joked that she fancied Noel. A joke, but it had been tasteless and it had cut Shelley to the quick. Imagine if her mum got off with Noel! Married him! Ugh! It would spoil things between her and Liam if that were to come to pass. No way. Noel would have more taste than that.

There wasn't enough here. She'd be hungry again soon. Tonight she'd go down to the chippy. Jimmy Mulgrew would be there. He was okay, but she didn't fancy him. He was too real, too here. Too Rosewell. He was awkward. Jimmy never knew the right things to say, like Alan Devlin at the garage did, or like Liam would. Okay, so Liam was from somewhere just like Rosewell really, but he had moved on, had shown that he had what it took to become a star. But she'd go to the chippy anyway, and then get home for *The X-Files*.

8

Jimmy and Semo were hanging around on the corner outside the chippy. The pubs were ready to lose in half-an-hour.

Jimmy wanted some chips but he and Semo had been barred by Vincent, the proprietor, for previous acts of minor theft and vandalism. Jimmy's heart rose when he saw Shelley and Sarah walking towards them. Shelley gave him a coy smile and Jimmy felt something move inside of him. He wanted to tell her how he felt, but what could he say? Here, in front of Semo and Sarah. What could he say to this tall, slender beauty who kept him awake at nights and who had been responsible for his sheets becoming as stiff as a board since she had flowered in the last few months and had got a number one like that Sinead O'Connor lassie? This called for genuine courtship, not darkened gropes down the quarry with the likes of Abby Ford and Louise Moncur whom he and Semo had christened 'The Reservoir Dogs'. But how could he ask her out? Where could they go? The pictures? The botanics? Where did you take lassies on proper dates?

Inspired by the shining moon overhead, which illuminated the obelisk of the office block above the garage, Jimmy moved towards her. – Eh, Shelley, goan git ays some chips, ah'll gie ye the money likes. Vincent's only went n barred us, eh.

– Awright then, Shelley said, taking the money from him.

– Mind n git sauce curry oan thum Shel, he smiled, chuffed at her not registering negatively at his referring to her in that more intimate and informal way.

They watched the girls move into the chip shop. – Two fuckin wee rides but, eh? Semo observed, parting his dry lips with a darting tongue and rubbing at the swelling on his jaw. – Ah'd shag thum baith, he hissed, then he grabbed Jimmy and gave him a theatrical pelvic hump.

Inside the chip shop Sarah turned to Shelley, – They're fuckin daft! Supposed tae be sixteen! They wouldnae ken what tae dae wi a real woman! The girls sniggered at the image of the boys through the shop window as they jostled and rucked with each other in nervous excitement.

9

The craft was many millions of light years from the Earth, and many millions more from its native solar system. Its occupants could witness, through the technology the Cyrastorian youth so professed to enjoy, images of the planet in great clarity. They knew that it was almost as effective as the pictures they could see through The Will, but this was easier and lazier. It gave the Cyrastorian Youngers and their solitary Earth friend time to enjoy a fag.

— Been a few fuckin changes wi the boys since ah wis steyin oan Earth, the ex-Hibs casual Mikey Devlin said to Tazak, the Cyrastorian youth's leader, as the monitor on the ship panned the East Stand at Easter Road.

— Ah kin bet mate, the tall, gangling Tazak replied, puffing on his Regal King Size. This substance called snout, that his stumpy Earthling friend whom he towered over, had introduced them to; it was a truly wondrous experience. He remembered that first time, when he had coughed up his virgin lungs. Now he was a forty-a-day creature.

Mikey scrutinised the faces, zeroing in on a few recognisable ones. — That wee cunt Ally Masters, used tae run wi the Baby Crew. Looks like ehs a top boy now. Nae fuckin sign ay the wee brar bit, eh.

Tazak smiled at his friend. — Well, we pey these cunts a visit the night. See what thir up tae, eh.

Mikey knew what that familiar glow in his friend's large brown eyes meant. He was up for some serious mischief. But there was a bigger issue. The time was at hand. His time, their time, and Tazak's adventurism could not be allowed to fuck things up. Whether you were in space with internal or external technology at your disposal which could obliterate solar systems, or on the streets with chibs or bottles, it was timing that was important. Mikey Devlin was a top boy. He knew the same rules applied anywhere in warfare. – Ah'm playin it cool first mind, ah'll stey up here until ye git the cunts tae see things oor wey. Then ah'll come doon. Once they fuckin tubes see who organised the whole deal, they'll accept me as the main man. N wir no jist talkin aboot the cashies here. Wir talkin the whole fuckin Planet Earth ya cunt.

– As long as this fuckin scam ay yours works oot ya cunt, a smile played across Tazak's small mouth, as he held his Regal King Size in his long, thin, fingers.

– Course it will. Wir no jist joy-ridin here, gaun doon thair n takin some cunts in thir sleep n stickin fuckin tubes up thir erses fir the crack. This is when we formally announce oor presence. This is whaire we brek aw yir Cyrastorian rules. Youse goat the boatil?

– Too right wi fuckin huv, Tazak said, somewhat defensively.

– You ken the auld cunts back it your place. They dinnae study Earth in great detail any mair. They ken it'll soon be fucked, eh. Aw they want is for you cunts no tae interfere, jist leave thum alain. But if youse go in and install ma crew as top boys oan the planet, then yis kin rule fae a distance and these auld cunts'll pick up fuck all sign ay any ay youse extra terrestrial radges doon oan earth. That's goat tae be the game plan, man.

— Sounds awright n theory . . . Tazak puffed on his tab.

Mikey smiled, flashing his large teeth at the young Cyrastorian. This was a gesture his friend, accustomed as he was to the Earthman's startling appearance, never found less than disturbing. — It's mair thin awright! Listen tae me ya cunt! Ah wis the cunt thit organised Anderlecht in the EUFA Cup.

— That's fuckin nowt tae this but, Tazak replied.

— It's the same fuckin thing; a city, Brussels, or a planet, Earth. Jist fuckin specs in the solar system.

— Suppose, Tazak conceded. He had to defer to the maturity of the Earth casual. This had been a worrying development recently.

It had been some time since they struck up their unlikely friendship. Tazak had been a novice Younger on a ship of Elders who had been sent on an errand to randomly pick one Earthling whom they would study and learn Earth language and culture from. The Earthling Mikey Devlin, was seized in an Edinburgh club when they had stopped Earth time, and he had, after a shock, proved to be only too willing to assist them. Mikey actually requested to extend his stay, wanted as he was by local police on Earth for a wounding offence at Waverley Station after a full-scale pagger.

Mikey Devlin had struck up a deal with the aliens. All they had to do was to go back to Earth with him on occasion, and find him some lassies to shag. The Elders were happy to oblige him. Mikey though, had befriended some of the alien youths, particularly Tazak, who would take him to Earth on their old cruising ship, enjoying his company. Mikey was a shrewd cunt and his stock had risen with the aliens and soon he became accepted as one of them. He encouraged the Youngers in the consumption of tobacco, a drug they seemed strongly pre-disposed towards. Their snout addiction kept them tied in a strange way to Planet Earth, and meant that Mikey would always be able to visit home. For his part, the only thing Tazak couldn't get used to was the rank, sweet smell of the Earth alien's skin.

Mikey thought that the aliens' naive interest in physical technology was a load of shite, and he had studied the power of The Will intensely, learning how to resource some of its wonders. He kept his disdain of the youths' interests to himself as he liked them and he had to concede that The Cyrastorian Elders were boring cunts.

10

The gathering of the posses and the tribes in the non-salubrious area of old Midlothian and south-east suburban Edinburgh had puzzled the travellers themselves as much as the authorities. Various new age sages and pseudo prophets had advanced their theories, but the local authorities could do nothing and the Government would not intervene as the population in the makeshift camps rose to over twenty thousand.

11

The local dealers were having a field day and Jimmy and Semo, high from an anticipated success with Clint Phillips in the criminal injuries scam, thought they'd try their hands at some more private enterprise. Semo had a good contact in Leith and they went into town in a nicked car to score some acid, in the hope of punting it to the travellers. They drove into the port and picked up their friend Alec Murphy, who took them down to a flat in the Southside, telling them that they were going to meet a guy whom Murphy simply referred to as 'The Student Cunt'.

– The Student Cunt's awright. Eh isnae really a student at aw, Alec explained. – He's no been tae a college or nowt like that fir years n years. Bit ehs goat a degree: economics, or some shite. But it's like, eh still sounds like a fuckin student, ken?

The boys nodded in a vague comprehension.

Alec warned them about The Student Cunt, whom, he felt, tended to formulate the most banal observations as rambling, philosophical propositions worthy of further speculation. On his day, Murphy observed, in optimum conditions, and in the right company, The Student Cunt could be mildly amusing. Such days, circumstances and companies were, he felt, increasingly few.

Mounting the steps of the dealers flat with growing anticipation and excitement, Jimmy Mulgrew felt that he had made the big time. He swaggered in like a gangster, checking his look in a mirror in the hallway. He would see Shelley down the chippy later, drop a few hints about 'business'. She couldn't fail to be impressed. Alan Devlin was yesterday's man, Jimmy thought, with a vigorous rush of confidence. A fuckin garage attendant! Top boy my hole! He'd lost it, and the cunt was just treading water. Jimmy's time had yet to happen.

Jimmy's fantasies deflated quickly as a guy with a mop of curly hair and black-rimmed glasses ushered them into the front room. There was a woman with lank brown hair and a vesty red top who was feeding a baby from a bottle. She didn't even register their presence.

– Alec . . . hi . . . said The Student Cunt, seeming a little put out at the observation of Alec's friends' relative youth. – Can I have a private word?

Alec turned back to Jimmy and Semo. – Hud oan a minute boys, he said, disappearing into the kitchen with The Student Cunt. Alec knew he shouldn't have brought them up to The Student Cunt's pad. He hadn't really been thinking.

– How old are these guys? The Student Cunt asked.

– Sixteen and seventeen, Alec said. – Young team, fae oot at Rosewell, but sound cunts like. Ah mean, ah mind you sais that ah could jist bring any cunt ah wanted sorted up here.

– That's all very well *ceteris paribus* Alec, The Student Cunt said, – but it's a truism that youth are always impressed by new things and therefore tend to run off at the fucking mouth and I can do without labdicks up my fucking arse.

– These boys ken the score, Alec shrugged.

The Student Cunt's eyes rolled doubtfully behind his spectacles.

In the living room, Jimmy was feeling the embarrassed silence with the mother and the baby. He reckoned Semo must have been too, because he was compelled to break it. – How auld's the bairn? he asked.

The woman looked up at him, her eyes cold and detached.

– Three months, she said disinterestedly.

Semo nodded thoughtfully. Then he pointed at the woman. – Listen, see whin ye hud the bairn, he asked, – wis it sair?

– What? The woman looked at him in a more focused manner.

– Whin ye hud the bairn, wis it sair?

She looked him up and down. Jimmy gave an involuntary

snigger, feeling as if a small motor which he couldn't switch 'off' was oscillating his shoulders from a space in his chest cavity.

— Naw, Semo began seriously, — it's jist, like, ah cannae imagine what it must be like tae huv tae dae something like that . . . it's too freaky, eh. Ah mean, ye cannae really think aboot a livin thing growin inside ay ye, cause it wid like freak ye oot, ken what ah mean?

— Ye just git on wi it, the woman shrugged.

— Ye jist git oan wi it, Semo repeated, nodding reflectively. Then he turned to Jimmy, — Ah suppose ye fuckin well huv tae, eh! He laughed. — Cannae take it back! He looked at the woman — It's true bit, eh?

Jimmy started sniggering again, as the woman on the couch shook her head and picked a bit of fluff out of the baby's ear. The Student Cunt came through, and, with a startled, apologetic expression aimed at the woman, ushered the boys from the Rosewell young team through to the kitchen.

Alec winked at them as The Student Cunt opened a cupboard, pulled out a bowl marked SUGAR, lifted a bag from it, and produced some tabs from the bottom.

— Fifty strawberries, he smiled.

— Sound, Jimmy smiled, and settled up.

They went back through to the living room and sat down. The Student Cunt put a tape on. As it started, Jimmy stole a glance at the woman with the baby, then clamped his jaw shut to stop himself from sniggering. He just vibrated softly on the couch.

The Student Cunt thought that Jimmy was vibing to the music. — East Coast Project, he said, then turning to Alec, added with great sincerity — Some pri-tay interesting things going down there.

– Mmm, Alec said non-committally.

The Student Cunt then turned to Semo. – Your neck of the woods, that's were all those posses have gathered, isn't it?

The woman feeding the baby looked up with interest for the first time.

– Aye, Semo nodded. – It's fuckin too radge.

This was The Student Cunt's cue to launch into a spiel concerning his view of what was happening in contemporary society. It was the others' cue to make their excuses and go. Jimmy winced when he heard The Student Cunt describe himself to Alec as 'working class', making it sound like 'wehking closs'. They departed as quickly as they could, going onto a snooker club for a couple of frames and a few beers. Then Alec left, so they thieved another motor to get back out to the sticks.

In the car, Jimmy couldn't resist trying one of the tabs. After a short time, the whole place seemed to go crazy and he could barely see Semo sitting next to him in the driver's seat.

– Just as well you never took any ay these Semo, Jimmy gasped, as the car turned and sped down the city roads into a wall of blinding light which shot up from the cat's eyes. They were flying. – Ah'm sayin, jist as well you never hud yin, eh Semo?

– Shut the fuck up . . . ah'm tryin tae concentrate oan the road . . . ah necked yin ay they tabs n aw n it's kickin in fine style! Semo moaned.

– STOAP! STOAP THE FUCKIN CAR! Jimmy felt the unremitting pulse of raw terror in every cell of his body.

– Fuck off! Ah kin see fine. Dinnae fuckin nudge ays! Semo snapped as Jimmy gripped his arm, – Ah kin see by the cat's eyes in the road . . . pit oan the fuckin cassette . . .

Jimmy clicked on the play button.

and all the roads that lead you there are winding
and all the lights that mark your path are blinding

– GIT THAT OAF! Semo roared. – Switch oan the fuckin radio!

– Right . . . Jimmy shivered. He switched on the radio.

and all the lights that mark your way are blinding
there are just so many things that I could say to you

– Ah sais switch it oaf! Pit oan the fuckin radio! Semo hissed.

– Ah did! That is the radio! It's oan the fuckin radio n aw! Same song!

– Fuck sakes . . . how mad is that man, eh? Semo groaned. He couldn't stop the car. Try as he might, he couldn't stop it. – This fuckin car willnae fuckin well stoap!

Jimmy had his hands over his eyes. He looked through them. They weren't moving. – It . . . it hus stoaped. Wir no movin. Wir stoaped ya daft cunt!

Semo realised that he had parked the car by the side of the road. They got out and made their way tentatively down the street. Everything seemed to be distorted, it was like everything was an effort. Just to keep walking. Just to keep moving. Then they stopped dead.

12

Tazak and Mikey walked down the three dimensional photograph that was Princes Street, absorbing the frozen stillness of the humans, their pets and their vehicles.

Mikey observed some girls, shopping smiles caught in suspended animation. – Hmmm . . . no bad . . .

This was one of the best things in this space game for Mikey Devlin: to just stop Earth time and check every cunt out. Tazak was getting impatient though. It was too much of a psychic energy outlay and it could even send a vibe to The Elders who would investigate and their game would be up before it really started. The best way to halt Earth time, was to pick a small, rural spot at night and freeze proceedings in the locality. Operating on this sort of scale was crazy. Tazak was growing irritated with Mikey's fannying about. – C'moan ya cunt! he shouted, – Wuv goat tae fuckin nash!

– Aye . . . aye . . . Mikey was looking a slim dark-haired girl up and down. – No bad, he commented, – no bad at aw.

Tazak stared with disgust at this chunky, hairy Earth female, with its ugly strips of fur above its tiny eyes; its weird head, with its large, protruding nose and that horrible swelling around the lips of the big mouth. They were truly a repulsive looking race, yet biologically not so different from his own people. He remembered back to his studies at The Foundation as a lesser, where the others had mocked his small eyes and called him 'The Earthling'. It was ironic that he should be down here now, mixing with them.

He shuddered in recall at the occasion, when, with Mikey, he had coupled with one of these creatures, a small, almost hairless female. They were all in a very high transcendental state at the time, but he had felt disgusted with himself afterwards. Even more irritated by this recall, he hissed at his Earth host, – Ah sais nash! Wuv goat things tae dae!

– Aye, right then ya cunt, Mikey moaned. He had to concede, there *were* things to do.

13

Shelley was dreaming again. She was on the ship and the alien was standing over her. There was a man there this time, a human being. It wasn't Liam. It looked a little bit like Alan Devlin.

14

Ally Masters was having the dream also. He was coming home with Denny McEwan and Bri Garratt through the city centre. Sole Fusion had been a good one but the fanny werenae biting and, if the truth be told, the E's were a bit smacky. He was feeling them. Everything seemed to be slowing down. Then, through a blurred haze Ally felt himself walk towards this strange light. It was more than an inappropriate appreciation of a distant streetlamp brought on by the pills. This was an amorphous mass of protoplasm and he was heading through it, it seemed to be forming a structure around him. He sensed that others were walking alongside him, but he couldn't turn his head. He tried to shout to Denny and Bri but nothing came out.

Then, in a strange instant he found himself fully awake and in what seemed like an immense white amphitheatre.

– Is this the fuckin whitey tae end aw whitey's or what? Ally asked, looking at Bri and Denny. His friends' eyes had shrank to pinpricks. He felt a strong ammonia-like sting in his nostrils.

– No fuckin real man! Denny said, tentatively touching the

white walls which had looked smooth but on closer examination and touch, seemed to be composed of tightly-packed glowing encrustations.

Then, where there had previously only seemed to be a wall, a door opened and two large aliens, naked save for a loin cloth to cover their genitals, and devoid of bodily hair, walked into the huge amphitheatre. – Awright boys. How yis daein? one of them asked.

The Earth thugs were too shocked to reply. Then, without looking at his friends, Bri Garratt asked, – Aw fuckin hell man . . . what the fuck've wi goat here . . .

– Fuckin aliens man! Wild! Denny McEwan gasped.

– Well fuckin aliens or nae fuckin aliens, nae cunt fucks wi the Hibs crew, Ally snarled, then turned to the Cyrastorian youths. – . . . ah dinnae ken what youse cunts are aboot, but if yis fuckin well want bother yis uv came tae the right fuckin place . . . The East Terracing Top Boy pulled out his stanley knife and advanced towards the tall, thin creatures.

The aliens remained unfazed by Ally Masters' approach. The Earth Casual sensed his hosts' dismissive arrogance. He lashed out at the spokesperson, only to feel his blade bounce against an invisible wall which the Hibs Boy could just about visualise as a quivering and pulsing translucent membrane, just a few inches from his would-be-victim.

– Yir shitey fuckin stanley knives are fuck all use against oor force field, eh Earth cunt! the alien sneered.

– Fuck . . . Ally moaned.

– No sae fuckin wide now, ya fuckin earth tube, another alien laughed.

The top alien gestured languidly and the stanley knife tore out of Ally's grip and stuck in the wall. – See Earth cunt, youse think thit yir a hard crew but yir jist a bunch ay fuckin shitein cunts in the whole intergalactic scheme ay things. We've no even started here yit. Whaire's yir top boys hing oot?

— What the fuck dae youse cunts want? Ally demanded.

— You tae shut yir mooth fir a second, the alien smiled through his thin lips. — Ah'm Tazak, by the way. Ah ken youse cunts so dinnae bother wi the introductions. Tazak lit up a cigarette. — Ah'd crash the ash, bit ah'm runnin a wee bit low. Anywey, here's how it is; thir's nae fuckin wey that youse cunts'll run us, dinnae even think aboot it. But we're here tae help youse. We need cunts doon here tae run the fuckin show fir us. We want youse cunts, cause youse speak oor fuckin language. Could've landed in California in the desert like in aw they crap films ay yours, but we went tae Midlothian but, eh.

— How here but? Masters asked.

— Goat tae land somewhere. Might as well be here as anywhere else, eh. Besides, we ken the score. It's only Scotland. Nae cunt listens tae youse dippit fuckers. Anywey, we'll make every cunt listen tae us. Whae runs things doon here now?

— Like, the main men n that? Ally asked.

— Aye.

— Well, that's like in London, or Washington, eh, Denny turned to Ally, who nodded.

— Fuck off, these cunts dinnae rule us, Bri tapped his chest.

— Aye, but that's the fuckin Government ya cunt. Like Westminster . . . or The White Hoose. That's whaire the real power is.

— The only fuckin White Hoose ah ken is the one in Niddrie . . . Denny laughed.

Tazak was growing impatient. — Shut it the now Earth

cunt! Wir talkin serious business here! We'll fuckin gie they cunts a wee demonstration ay what we kin dae. They kin pit the polis oan as much fuckin OT as they like . . . this is the mentalist crew in the universe thir dealin wi here! They've no seen real fuckin swedgin yit! We'll fuckin show thum swedgin! Swedgin thit could tear a fuckin solar system apart!

The top boys looked at each other. This alien cunt, this Tazak, talked a good pagger. They would bide their time and see if the cunt could deliver. They could feel the adrenaline pumping through their bodies. Masters and his crew sensed that they had been preparing themselves all their lives for something like this to go off, and they were determined not to let the colours down.

15

The chippy was doing great business. Not from the travellers who were barred by the growing number of police from crossing over the fly-over, but from the reporters and camera crews who had come to observe the phenomenon. However, Vincent, the proprietor, was still a far from happy man. There had been a break-in the other night. The fags and cash had been secured in a strongroom and the lock was intact. The thieves, in their frustration at only being able to get some confectionery, had splashed the contents of industrial sized chip sauce containers all over his shop. He had an idea who the culprits were. It had to be that Ian Simpson and that Jimmy Mulgrew. He'd see Drysdale about this.

16

The energy was there. It was telling them to come to Scotland. In London, in Amsterdam, in Sydney, in San Francisco, the posses on their comedowns heard the message. They would all head to Rosewell in Midlothian for the greatest ever gathering of human spirits. The energy crackled in the air. Posse leaders, seemingly driven, pointed the way to this small settlement on the fringes of Northern Europe. The authorities, sensing something was in the air, watched and waited.

At the chippy, Vincent is dumbfounded. The lock for the strongroom is intact and the cash is all there, but the cigarettes miraculously seem to have vanished.

17

It's almost 4.00 am and Andrew, Jimmy's dad, feels that his son should be asleep and his mates should be home, instead of upstairs in Jimmy's room playing those cheap Tartan Techno tapes which they buy in the Asian Discount Stores up the South Bridge. Parental control had become a blurred concept since Jimmy had filled out and met his old man's warning gazes with challenging, hardened eyes.

Jimmy's dad is not too sensitive though, and as long as it's low enough for him to hear the satellite telly, then it's not a problem. The Doctor's valium has taken the edge off Andrew's pain. His wife is long gone. She got fed up with Andrew's depression, impotence and lack of cash since his redundancy from Bilston Glen and went to live with a Day Centre worker in Penicuik.

Jimmy should be sleeping. Fuckin school, Andrew thinks, then remembers that his son left last year. Andrew feels that Jimmy's mother must be giving their son money. Money which goes on drugs when Andrew finds himself lucky to manage a fuckin pint down the club on a giro day. That selfish wee cunt and his mates were always off their tits on something or other. Like the other night; they had come back in some state. Acid. He knew what it was. These wee cunts thought that they had invented drugs.

It's ten years since he was made redundant from the pit. History had vindicated Scargill, sure, but that counted for fuck all. The times had been about selfishness and greed and Scargill was simply out of time and Thatcher was in. Andrew had put in his shift on the picket lines, went on demos, but had sensed from the off that it wasn't going to be a glorious time for the old industrial proletariat. The vibe was important. The vibe then was small and petty and fearful, with too many people eager to brace the false certainties their masters and assorted lackeys bleated out.

In a way it was healthier now: nobody believed in anything these lying bastards ever spouted. Even the politicians themselves seemed to rap out the old bullshit with more desperation than the traditional smug conviction we'd grown accustomed to. The vibe was changing alright, but what was it changing into?

Boom boom boom. The tartan techno beat thudded insistently. Boom boom boom. Andrew hit the volume button on the handset, but the fuckin tartan techno, it was moving up too, keeping pace. Then Mrs Mooney next door was thumping on the wall. Andrew let his knuckles go white on the rests of the chair.

Upstairs, Jimmy and the boys are celebrating. The duty

cop at the sub-station, PC Drysdale had given them the coveted crime number they required to advance their Criminal Injuries Claim. Dysdale had taken in the young team's fictitious rantings all too eagerly. He had little time for the local yobs, but far less for those fucking travellers who were making life on his patch a complete misery. It would only take one flashpoint incident for something horrendous to go off, then his promotion board chances would be well and truly jeopardised. Drysdale's instincts told him to wade in and bang up some likely-looking crusties. This sensitive policing bollocks had its limitations. However, he knew the line that Cowan, the head guy on the promotion board would be taking.

18

The Hibs Boys were being less than co-operative with the aliens. – How the fuck should we help youse? Ally Masters asked Tazak.

The alien puffed thoughtfully on his cigarette. – Youse kin dae what yis fuckin well like . . .

He was interrupted by another voice: – Cause we're daein you a favour ya fuckin radge! A human figure stepped out from the shadows and the Earthlings stood shocked at the presence of one of their own kind.

The Hibs Boys started in disbelief. It was Mikey Devlin, Alan Devlin's brother. The cunt that had vanished. Now he was back. He was still clad in Nike's!

– Mikey Devlin! Ally Masters said, looking Mikey up and

down. – Very . . . eh, eighties gear, ma man. The trainers like. Whaire ye been hidin?

– Hyperspace, eh, Mikey smiled, – N ah've goat a tale tae tell youse cunts thit's a loat mair important thin fuckin labels.

He told the boys the story.

– But how could ye just leave like that? Bri Garratt demanded.

– Turn yir back oan yir mates? Ally asked.

– Turnt ehs back oan Scotland, Denny McEwan sneered.

The parochialism of his old crew was getting on Mikey's tits. – Fuck Scotland ya daft cunt! Ah've been aw ower the fuckin Universe! Seen things youse cunts couldnae fuckin well see in yir wildest dreams!

– Fuck it Mikey. Dinnae come back here n slag off Scotland, that's aw ah'm sayin, Denny held his ground.

Mikey looked tiredly at Tazak. These cunts were just not getting the message. – Scotland . . . he scoffed. – It's jist a fuckin spec ay dust tae me. Shut the fuck up aboot Scotland. Ah'm back here tae make us the top fuckin crew oan Planet Earth!

19

The weather had broken. It pished rain from the heavens. Trevor Drysdale tried to get a good night's sleep for his promotion board interview the next day. Only the thoughts of those crusty bastards, drenched in a cold field gave him the warm satisfaction to lull him into a soft dreamland. As anxious as he was the next morning, Drysdale had prepared well. Interviews were all about cracking codes, finding the current vogue; one minute liberal rhetoric, the next the hard line. The best professional in any bureaucracy was always the one who could control his or her prejudices and learn the dominant spiel with conviction. How one acted, of course, was totally irrelevant, as long as the espousal was effective. With Cowan, it was the liberal bullshit he wanted, so Drysdale would give him it, in shovel loads. For Cowan, this was almost as important as personal tidiness.

20

Clint Phillips had been body-swerving Jimmy and Semo since his hospital discharge and the registration of the crime with PC Drysdale. They meet up with Dunky by the quarry, who tells them that Clint has intimated to them that he does not intend to share out the proceeds from the Criminal Injuries Compensation Board. Jimmy and Semo decide to put the frighteners on Clint. They will steal a car and drive it at high speed at him, across the forecourt in the garage. – Show the cunt wir no fuckin aboot here, Semo said.

21

Trevor Drysdale looks at his reflection in the mirror. He has back-combed and blow-dried his hair. He looks a bit poofy with a quiff, Drysdale thinks, but Cowan would approve of the softer image, which is much less severe than his normal brylcreamed look. Drysdale considers that he cuts quite a dash in his light grey Moss Bros suit. He was moving out of this ugly hell-hole, taking on supervisory responsibilities. The South Side Area station was calling.

Drysdale notes that the heavy rain had stopped. He takes the car into the city, allowing himself plenty of time. He parks about half-a-mile away from that huge, pristine, structure; a true temple of law enforcement, that is the South Side Area station. Drysdale elects to walk, so that he can come upon the building that will surely be his new home, to orientate himself slowly and gradually to his new surroundings.

22

Jimmy and Semo's attempted scare on Clint was a failure. As they parked in waiting across the road, Clint was nowhere to be seen. Instead, Jimmy's anger rose as he saw Shelley and Sarah go into the garage and disappear into the back shop with Alan Devlin.

— That Devlin cunt . . . Jimmy hissed.

— Hud on the now, Semo smiled, — we'll show that fucker.

Alan Devlin was fucking Sarah across the table, and Shelley was watching them, thinking how uncomfortable it looked as to how it felt when her and Alan were actually doing it.

Devlin was well into his stride when a loud, repetitive car horn blasted from the forecourt. — Fuck! Marshall! He snarled, pulling out of a tense Sarah, who tugged her skirt down and her knickers on in almost one movement. Devlin janked on his trousers and ran into the front shop. Jimmy and Semo were in the car, with the window wound down. They were waving bags of crisps and some other stock they had taken from the shop while Devlin had been on the job.

– YOUSE UR FUCKIN DEID YA WEE CUNTS! Alan growled, charging towards the car, but the boys sped off down the road.

At this point Clint came across the forecourt, licking an ice cream cone.

– Whair the fuck've you been? Devlin hissed.

– Ah jist goat a cone . . . fae the van . . . Clint gasped weakly, as Shelley and Sarah giggled in the shop doorway.

– Ah fuckin well telt ye tae keep shoatie! Devlin snapped, and in a swiping movement knocked Clint's cone from his hand onto the oily forecourt.

The younger man's face flushed red and his eyes watered as he registered the chuckles emanating from the girls.

Jimmy and Semo had decided to keep the car and go into town to score more drugs. They had managed to successfully punt the acid to a posse of travellers. The stolen car, a white nissan micra, was, by co-incidence, exactly the same colour and year as that driven by Allister Farmer, a member of the local police promotion board for the South Side of Edinburgh. The co-incidence became a cruel one as Farmer, heading up to the South Side Area office to conduct some promotion interviews, was overtaken by Jimmy and Semo's car as they sped up into town to head down to Alec Murphy's at Leith.

Having passed Farmer, Jimmy giving the outraged plain-clothed cop a languid V-sign, they tore up St Leonard's Street. As Trevor Drysdale was walking along the pavement, thinking of his responses to the questions that would be asked at the interview, he was unawares that he was passing a huge, murky, oily puddle which spilled onto the road from a blocked drain. Drysdale had little time to react as a white nissan micra sent a sheet of filthy liquid flying over him. In an instant Drysdale's quiff was plastered to his cranium, and one side of the light grey suit had turned a wet black.

Drysdale could only look himself up and down. He let out an anguished, primal scream from the depths of his sickened soul: – YA BASTARD! YA FUCKEN BASTARD!! as he looked up to see the back of the white micra recede up the street.

The police promotional applicant was unawares however, that there were two white nissan micras, and that the offending one had got through the lights at the top of the road. However, the second one, containing the innocent Allister Farmer, had stopped at red. Farmer had been so full of anger at the careless driving in the car ahead, that he hadn't noticed what had happened to the unfortunate pedestrian on St Leonard's Street.

On noticing that the lights had changed to red and that the micra had halted, Drysdale embarked on a lung-bursting run towards the stationary car. On catching up to it, he tapped the side window. Allister Farmer rolled it down, only to be met with a choking throaty roar of: – YOU FUCKIN BASTARD! and a clenched fist, which crashed into him, bursting his nose.

Drysdale was off. He had extracted his revenge, now he had to save the situation. He still had ten minutes left. He ran into a pub and attempted to clean himself up as best he could. He looked at his image in the mirror. He was a mess, an absolute fucking mess. All he could do was to try and explain to Cowan, and hope that the chairman of the promotion board would accept his story and turn a blind eye to his appearance.

Allister Farmer stemmed the blood with a hanky. The police inspector was shaken. He had investigated many such arbitrary assaults, but had never ever conceived of himself as the victim of one, particularly in broad daylight, on a busy road, outside a main police station. Farmer had been too stunned to see where the culprit had escaped to. He shakily started up his car, passed through the lights and parked outside the Area office.

— Allister! What happened? Are you okay? a concerned Tom Cowan asked, as a first aider treated Farmer's nosebleed. A couple of investigating officers were straight outside, looking for the culprit.

— God Tom, I was assaulted, in my own car, just outside the bloody station, by some fucking community care jakey who tapped on my window . . . anyway . . . we've got our interviews. The show must go on.

— What did the guy look like?

— Later Tom, later. Let's not keep the interviewees waiting.

Cowan nodded affirmatively, ushering Farmer and Des Thorpe from personnel into the interview room. They had another quick look at the forms they had already studied in detail. In terms of experience, background and lodge membership, they agreed that Trevor Drysdale was an excellent candidate for one of the posts. — I know Drysdale, Cowan said, brushing a distasteful white thread off his jacket sleeve. — A craft stalwart and a damn fine polisman.

They sent for Drysdale who trooped timidly in. Cowan's jaw fell, but not as far as Farmer's.

On noting who was on the interview panel, Drysdale just

covered his eyes and burst into tears. Another decade at the sub-station loomed.

23

Gezra, the Appropriate Behaviour Compliance Elder, found it hard to fathom today's youngsters. He had, perhaps, been around too long, he considered again, but what satisfaction they got from going to backward places like Earth in their beat-up space crafts and kidnapping hapless aliens and sticking anal probes into them was beyond his understanding. It was just one of these things that youths did, he supposed. Once it got into the culture and telepathic media got a hold of it, it spread like a bush fire. These kids were harmless really, but the animals on Earth had rights too, something it was difficult for youngsters nowadays to grasp.

His people had learned all about Earth culture from a native of the planet called Mikey Devlin, whom they had kidnapped for cultural study five years ago. He opted to stay with them rather than undergo memory wipe, provided they could supply him with young Earth women, the dangerous and highly addictive substance called snout, and the odd take-away. Several top Hollywood actresses and international models, *Sun* page three girls and females who frequented Buster Browns niteclub in Edinburgh had claimed that aliens had come for them in the night, but nobody made the connection or took the complaints seriously. They all said that one of the creatures looked human. Well that was Devlin, thought the Appropriate Behavioural Compliance Officer: a fanny merchant of the first order.

Mikey had been okay when he stuck to the official tours. He was sound, a plausible cunt, and they liked having him around. But, Gezra reflected, the Earthman had fallen in with a crowd of rebellious youngsters and they took him on trips back home. They weren't bad really, but they were silly. Once they entered the procreative years, this behaviour would cease. Of course, by then, there would be a new team to worry about. But for now, the Earthman was with them. Gezra was concerned that Mikey might try to tempt them to make contact with his old friends on Earth. This was strictly forbidden without a memory wipe. So it had to be Earth. Tazak and Mikey would need to replenish snout supplies. He would go there by technology, to avoid being detected, rather than by The Will. He set his controls.

24

Jimmy and Semo were unable to score anything from Alec other than some Temazapam capsules and a little bit of hash. They were pretty disappointed as they drove back out from the city.

25

And all the people who had converged on the fields near the old mine workings, people for as far as could be seen, were listening to the music, the sweet music which filled the air, and feeling the exhilarated rushes as the sky darkened by the awesome sight of the craft coming down to earth. It hovered some seventy feet above them.

The ship, in its magnificent splendour, did not move. It just stayed put. This was it, this was the moment the travellers had been waiting for.

26

Jimmy and Semo first noticed delays at the Newcraighall Roundabout. Then the police were turning everyone back. — But we live ower thair, Semo pleaded, lost to the fact that they were in a stolen car. The cop had other things on his mind. He pointed over to the huge disc that hung in the sky over the other side of the bypass.

— Thir's a fuckin flying saucer oan toap ay ma hoose, Semo turned to Jimmy.

27

At the hastily convened conference in Washington, the world's leaders were finding it difficult to understand the alien spokespersons. They had enlisted some of the CCS top boys, who had the confidence of the aliens, to help with the translation.

— We could fuckin run youse like that, Tazak snapped his fingers. — Aw yir fuckin weapons, thir fuckin nowt against us, eh.

The world leaders looked far more concerned than the

impassive, square-jawed security men from the federal forces, who surrounded them.

— Fuckin shitein cunts, another alien sneered, picking up on the psychic vibe of fear.

— I don't see that this . . . the British Prime Minister started.

— You shut yir fuckin mooth ya specky cunt! Tazak snapped. — Nae cunt's fuckin talkin tae you! Right! Fuckin wide-o!

The PM looked nervously at his feet. A Special Air Services Officer who flanked him, tensed up.

— What ah wis fuckin sayin before this cunt started wis, Tazak looked at the PM who was silent, — we could fuckin annihilate youse in a swedge. Nae fuckin problem. We've goat the fuckin technology, eh. And the fuckin willpower. So the wey we see is, youse cunts dae as yis ur fuckin well telt and that's it. Endy fuckin story.

Ally from the CCS stood up. For all that they spoke the same language, the alien's arrogance still jarred. If only he could get that cunt with his force-field down. — No in a square go yis couldnae.

— Eh? What's this cunt sayin? one alien asked Tazak.

The American President put his hand on Ally's shoulders to force him to sit down. — Sit on your ass godamn you, they got us over a barrel!

Ally's head crashed into the leader of the western world's nose. The President fell back into his chair. A security man from the FBI moved forward but the alien raised his hand and the President ushered him to stop.

— Nae cunt fuckin pills me up, Ally said.

— Boy's right enough, Tazak considered. — Ah'm hearin a loat ay talk fae youse cunts aboot this n that, but these boys are the only ones that huv stuck up fir thumselves. He looked at Ally, – Yir no tryin tae tell me thit youse cunts ur feart ay they cunts, his large almond eyes sweeping over the world's leaders.

– That'll be fuckin right, Ally said, looking challengingly at the late middle-aged posse of suits who led the world.

– Bit these cunts are the top boys, they tell every cunt what tae dae but, Tazak said.

The Chancellor of the German Federal Republic cut in, – But ziss is a democracy. Ze process of choosink leaders is not based on physical fighting abilities but on ze vill of all ze people.

– Is it fuck, Ally said, quickly putting the cunt right, – If that's right, he said, pointing at the British Prime Minister, – how is it that nae cunt in Scotland voted for these bastards and we git thaim rulin us? Answer ays that! If ye fuckin well kin!

– Right enough, said Bri. Then he turned to the German Chancellor, – You keep yir fuckin nose oot ay things ye ken nowt aboot, right?

There followed a series of loud arguments. At one stage, it looked as if it was going to go off between the top boys of the Capital City Service and the security forces of the FBI.

– Fuckin shut it! Tazak, the alien top boy shouted, pointing at the world's leaders. – Listen, ah cannae handle they radge cunts nippin ma heid. Fae now oan, he nodded over to the casuals, – youse cunts are in charge here. The alien leader threw a transmitter over to Ally. The startled football thug jumped back, letting the device drop on the floor. – It's only a fuckin mobby ya radge! Pick it up!

Ally tentatively picked up the transmitter.

– Wi that yis kin bell us at any time, day or night. See if

these cunts, he swept his hand contemptuously round at the world's leaders, – if they fuckin well gie yis any grief, just bell us and we'll sort the cunts right oot. Fuckin surein wi will. Sort the cunts oot fir good, eh.

– Sound, Ally smiled. – Listen though . . . youse cunts say thit yis kin destroy anything on Earth fae space wi yir weapons?

– Aye . . . yis ur welcome tae come aboard n huv a shot, eh.

28

From the alien ship, Mikey Devlin looked down on the thousands of ravers making their excited pilgrimage below. He willed the monitor to pan out, across the green and brown hills of the Pentlands, and over the cityscape.

Something had twinged in a corner of Mikey's psyche. He retraced, focusing on the by-pass, almost directly underneath them. He could see the garage. Closing up, Mikey was elated to spy his brother, Alan, operating the car wash.

Alan wanted to get rid of the driver, a PC Drysdale, as soon as possible. He had a young woman called Abigail Ford in a state of semi-undress in the back shop. Drysdale seemed away with it though. Probably this space thing had freaked him. Loads of them were like that. He had to concede that it was pretty mind-blowing. Mind you, with all this millennium shite, it was about time some cunts from outer space finally got round to checking us out. Then, at the corner of his eye, Alan saw something move in the front shop. He was concerned that Abby was getting ready to go. It wasn't her though, it was those wee wide cunts Jimmy Mulgrew and Semo!

– These cunts are robbin us! He shouted at Drysdale, who wouldn't react. Alan ran towards the shop, and Semo got out just in time, but he cornered Jimmy Mulgrew. The younger man tried to swing at him, but he was overpowered by the senior hoolie, who dragged him outside and proceeded to boot him all over the forecourt. Semo jumped on Devlin's back, but he was thrown off, and had to frantically scramble to his feet and swiftly retreat in order to escape a similar punishment to his friend.

Alan raked the battered young teamster's pockets and found only some change and a handful of jellies, which he confiscated. Drysdale drove out without making an arrest.

From his vessel, Mikey watched approvingly as his brother fucked the young girl in the back shop, as Jimmy Mulgrew stood up and staggered along the street. He waited until his brother had finished and the girl has departed, before freezing local time and carrying him onto the craft.

Alan was delighted to see his brother again. – Mikey! Ah dinnae belief it! You're behind aw this shite! Ah knew it! Ah'm no jokin man, somethin telt ays tae come tae this fuckin place! That was how ah couldnae leave here! It wis you man! He studied his older brother. – Fuck sake man, ye look younger thin me!

– Clean livin, Mikey smiled, – No like you ya cunt! It was useless to try to explain the concept of controlling cellular elasticity and form through the use of The Will.

– No goat any blaw, huv ye? Mikey asked.

– Naw, ah took some jellies oaf this wee cunt.

– What are they? Mikey asked with interest. As Alan

explained, Mikey's eyes grew wider with interest. He took some from Alan. – Jist ma fuckin ticket these, eh.

29

The day after the conference in Washington had effectively installed the Casual Administration as the new unitary Earth Government, there followed a series of disasters unprecedented in British sporting history. The board of directors of Heart of Midlothian FC were devastated to find that the stadium, which boasted three brand new stands had been completely vaporised by a beam from outer space. In Glasgow, Ibrox, so long Scotland's showcase arena, immediately suffered a similar fate. The next horror was the destruction of Wembley Stadium and its famous twin towers. Then, sequentially, all the football grounds in the country with the exception of Easter Road in Edinburgh, were obliterated. Ally and his mates made their centre for Earth Government at the stadium, using the funds of various Earth nation states to completely refurbish the ground and embark on a massively expensive team-building programme.

On the terraces, there were a few die-hards who whinged on about 'these fuckin casual cunts' in charge of the club, but generally the new regime was welcomed. The outgoing board had been even less happy than the International Heads of State in standing down in favour of the Top Boys, but had little option in face of the power the casual hoolies now wielded.

– Cool gig this, eh, Tazak said, as Mikey watched on the monitor. They still had made no contact with the dancing crowds below the craft. However, the time was nearly right.

– Aye, and it hus tae be said that they've done a better joab for the club than the cunts they hud in charge before. It's aw doon tae resources though, the eighties Top Boy sagely conceded.

Tazak looked at his friend. – Wi ready tae hit it?

30

Cheers went up from the dancing hordes below as a thrashing telepathic bass-line rocked the planet and the crowd jumped and swayed to a blinding series of lasers which shot out from the craft. An Earth voice, a Scottish voice, asked: 'are we havin a fuckin good one?' and the crowd screamed in unison: 'yes!' They certainly were, the only dissenting voices coming from the Fubar crew who were signalling for more. – Lenny Dee! some cunt shouted.

An opening appeared in the craft and a small balcony extended from it. An Earthman walked out onto it. A huge cheer was heard as his image was beamed for miles around. – We've goat the best fuckin sound system in the universe here! Mikey roared.

Shelley looked up from the crowd. This man was even more fantastic than Liam from Oasis . . . he was the man of her dreams.

At that point the man said: – And now gies a top planet Earth welcome tae this big, skinny, spammy cunt whae's made it aw possible! Fae acroas the cosmos, planet Cyrastor, massive respect for our fuckin main man, Tazaaaak!

Tazak joined Mikey on the balcony. He felt humbled by the

reception the Earth crowd gave. No way was the big alien cunt about to lose the floor with the stakes so high, and punters jumping about for as far as his large brown eyes could see. Vibing like fuck, he unleashed a psychic virus of beautiful and powerful sound unequalled anywhere in the universe.

The Earth crowd had known nothing like it. Even those who had been privileged to attend some of the biggest and most happening events since 1988's summer of love, had to concede that this one was a bit special. Even club snobs agreed that the almost non-existent toilet and catering facilities failed to put a downer on the awesome nature of this event.

When he was exhausted, Tazak brought it down, and staggered from the balcony, back into the craft, to a tumultuous reception. – Cheers . . . that's me fucked . . . he telepathically flashed to the hordes below.

Inside the craft, Mikey was devastated. This was to be his big moment, but there was no way he could match that. The Earth man went out and did his best, using the full range of the psychic powers he'd developed, even extending himself past his breaking point, but very quickly into his set some groups were already chanting for the return of the big alien. He cut his performance short and returned to the interior of the craft, totally humiliated.

– Good one, Mikey conceded to his show-stealing friend, as he entered the amphitheatre which was the craft's central Will propulsion temple.

– It wis the fuckin best! Ah fuckin blew these Earth cunts away! Tell ays that wisnae something else! Tazak roared triumphantly.

– Aye, right, Mikey moped.

Tazak turned to his friend. – Listen mate, you goat any snout oan ye? Ah'm gantin oan a fag, eh.

– Naw, Mikey said, reaching in his pocket and producing one of the jellies he'd taken from Jimmy. – Take one ay these.

– What are they? Tazak asked, examining the egg-shaped capsules.

– Thir jist pills. They take away the snout cravin until wi kin go doon and git sorted, eh, Mikey shrugged. His face twisted into a smile, when, from the corner of his eye, he saw the alien neck the capsule.

31

Tazak was still recovering from the gig when Ally, Denny and Bri came through a door into the craft's central Will propulsion chamber. There was another human with the casual mob. Tazak, who had grown used to differentiating members of the species, thought he looked like Mikey. The Cyrastorian glanced over at his human colleague. – What the fuck are these cunts daein here? They've no goat authorisation.

Mikey smiled. – Ah gied thum authorisation, but eh. That's ma brar, he nodded at Alan, who smiled at Tazak, showing a full set of Earth teeth like Mikey's.

– You dinnae fuckin gie nae cunt authorisation oan this fuckin ship Mikey! Tazak pointed at himself, – ah'm the only cunt that gies any cunt authorisation! Right!

Mikey stretched idly. – Naw, it's no right mate. Ye see, thir's gaunny be some fuckin changes roond here. This is ma fuckin ship now.

– Fuck off Piltonian, dinnae you start gittin wide oan ays, Tazak scoffed, as Mikey squared up to him.

– You're no the only cunt wi psychic powers Tazak. Mind that, Mikey warned.

Tazak laughed like a half-choked drain. This would be fuckin sad if wasn't so funny. It was time this so-called Top Boy was put in his place. – Huh, huh, huh! Ye saw what happened tae your psychic powers oot thair! Tazak sniggered, then turned to the Hibs crew and pointed to the hull of the craft. – Eh loast the fuckin flair! He shook his head forlornly at Mikey. – Listen Earth cunt, ah might have taught ye aw that you ken, bit ah nivir taught ye aw thit ah ken!

This was true. Despite his immersion into Cyrastorian culture, Tazak, with that show outside, had painfully demonstrated to Mikey that he had a repertoire and volume of psychic skills which the Hibs Boy could never hope to emulate.

However, the ex-CCS Top Boy had one trick up his sleeve. – See that fuckin pill ah gied ye the now? Fir the snout cravin?

Tazak looked hesitant. Mikey flashed his teeth. Ally and the other boys looked leery.

– Well it wis nowt tae dae wi fags. It wis a jelly. Any minute now, aw your psychic powers'll be fuckin useless, eh. The only Will you'll be able tae access'll be the one ah hope yuv made oot fir yir next ay kin, ya cunt!

At these words Tazak felt his senses spinning out of control. He tried to orientate himself through the exercise of The Will, but he was unsteady on his long legs – . . . ughn . . . feel . . . suddenly . . . cunted . . . he gasped, staggering backwards against the glistening, encrusted hull of the ship.

The Hibs boy seized his chance and decked the gangling, foal-like alien with a chunky fist to the side of the creature's face, toppling the frail Cyrastorian like a stacked tower of playing cards. – No sae fuckin wide now, ya fuckin streak ay alien pish! Lesson in life: nae cunt fucks wi the Hibees boys! The cosmic thug grinned arrogantly as he sank the boot into his old intergalactic comrade's skinny rib cage.

Ally Masters and the boys moved in for the kill. – Nice one Mikey! Lit's fuckin well stomp this cunt!

Mikey though, halted the advancing Hibs boys. He looked down at his friend, who was shaking, making a high, agonised noise that the Hibs hoolie had never heard before, and his skin was losing its indigo blue hue, becoming a sickly pink. – Leave um! The cunt's fucked!

Mikey backed away in horror from Tazak's high-pitched, resonant squeals which produced no intelligent words, although it was obvious the Cyrastorian was trying to speak them.

– What is it? Ally snapped.

– These cunts arenae used tae bein touched physically. That's how thir that weak lookin. They cannae survive withoot thir psychic shields! Ah've probably fuckin killed um! Mikey fell to his knees. – Tazak mate . . . ah'm fuckin sorry . . . ah didnae mean tae . . .

– Keep away from him!

Mikey turned to see an advancing Elder. He wore the white robes of the Appropriate Behaviour Control. Although this Cyrastorian looked the same as the rest of race to the other Top Boys, Mikey had learned to distinguish them and he knew this one. – Gezra . . . he whispered.

– You've caused a fair bit ay bother, eh Earth cunt . . .

– Ah didnae mean tae . . . Mikey stuttered.

The Appropriate Behaviour Control Elder had heard it all before. – Now it's time fir ye tae pey bit, eh.

The other Hibs Boys tried to run the Cyrastorian Elder, but there was nothing the football neds could do as light and sound burst and ripped all around them. They shut their eyes and held their ears to try to block out the shattering pain, but it seemed to be inside of them; twisting, ripping and splintering their bones. Unconsciousness mercifully took them, one by one, Ally Masters defiantly the last man to pass out.

32

Gezra had a lot of work to do. Firstly, Tazak had to be repaired, otherwise the youth would be reduced to the carrion phase, which was unacceptable. It had been centuries since any Cyrastorian had died before their allocated time span. Death was not appropriate behaviour for one so young. Fortunately, the reparations proved non-problematic for such an experienced master of The Will.

The next phase he needed help with, having to send for a Cyrastorian task force. This was unprecedented, but the behaviour of Mikey and Tazak meant that the entire inhabitants of Planet Earth needed memory wiping. It was a big job, and the Principal Elders at The Foundation would not be amused at this state of affairs.

33

Shelley woke up feeling as if her head was going to explode. Her guts were in a turmoil, and she had shooting, stabbing pains in her abdomen. She made her way unsteadily to the toilet, unsure of which orifice to put towards the bowl. In the end she sat on it and felt a sickening shudder followed by a violent excretion of the life she had within her. She fell to the floor, her blood trailing across the bathroom lino. Before she slid into unconsciousness, the young woman had the strength to pull the flush, so that she would never have to look at the matter she had miscarried.

Lillian heard the screams and was quickly at her daughter's side. Ascertaining that Shelley was still breathing, she ran downstairs and called an ambulance. When she got back to the bathroom, the young girl was semi-conscious. She looked at her mother and said, – Sorry mum . . . I didnae even like the boy . . .

– It's okay darlin, it's okay . . . Lillian wheezed in a soft mantra, moping her sick child's brow, awaiting the ambulance's arrival.

They took Shelley into the hospital, where they kept her for a few days. The Doctors told Lillian that she had had a miscarriage with some bad internal bleeding, but there would be no lasting damage. They advised her to put the girl on the pill. Lillian was too relieved to have strong words with her daughter; they would come later.

Sarah visited Shelley and told her that Jimmy was asking after her. Shelley was pleased to hear this. Jimmy was okay. Not as cool as Liam, but better than that Alan Devlin, who had just used her, getting her pregnant like that. She felt relieved. Whatever she told herself, she hadn't really wanted a baby.

34

Alan Devlin was upset when he re-discovered his brother Mikey, only to find that he had been sent to jail. The polis finally caught up with him for that wounding offence at Waverley Station, all those years ago. Alan jacked in the garage job, there seemed little point in hanging around such a dump as Rosewell. These wee lassies from the school were fuckin jailbait and he wanted none of that, he saw what prison was doing to his brother.

Alan had gone back into town, where he met a trendy woman from London at the Edinburgh Festival. He moved down to her place in Camden Town, and currently works behind a bar in Tufnell Park. He regularly returns to Edinburgh, to visit his brother Mikey in Saughton Prison, but he finds the visits very distressing. Mikey has lost his marbles a little, going on about aliens, who come to his cell in the night, and insert all sorts of probes into his orifices.

It hurts Alan to admit it, but he reckons that his brother has become a bit of a shirtlifter on the inside, and all this aliens stuff is just denial.

But in the chilling silence of frozen Earth time, Mikey's anguished soul screams its mute pleas for assistance and clemency as Tazak's crew remove his immobilised body from his cell, and take it to their craft for further investigation.

Back in Rosewell, Jimmy is excited; Clint has split the Criminal Injuries Compensation cash with them. It looks like him and Semo are up for Rezurrection this weekend, with Shelley and Sarah.

Started in 1992 by Kevin Williamson, with help from established young authors Duncan McLean and Gordon Legge, Rebel Inc. magazine set out with the intention of promoting and publishing what was seen then as a new wave of young urban Scottish writers who were kicking back against the literary mainstream.

The Rebel Inc book imprint intends to develop the magazine ethos through publishing accessible as well as challenging texts aimed at extending the domain of counter-culture literature.

The first four titles point towards the future direction of Rebel Inc

Children of Albion Rovers - Irvine Welsh, Alan Warner, Gordon Legge, James Meek, Laura J. Hird, Paul Reekie
A collection of novellas from six of the best young writers to emerge from Scotland in the 90s - £8.99
Hunger - Knut Hamsun - a new translation by Sverre Lyngstad with an introduction by Duncan Mclean
Classic first novel by the Nobel prize-winning Norwegian - £6.99

Young Adam - Alexander Trocchi - with an introduction by John Pringle
Seminal first work from the Scottish Beat writer - £6.99

Drugs and the Party Line - Kevin Williamson - with an introduction by Irvine Welsh
A polemic on the politics of recreational drug use - £4.99

The above are available from all good book shops or can be ordered direct from:

Canongate Books, 14 High St, Edinburgh EH1 3NX
Tel # 0131 557 5111 Fax # 0131 557 5211
email # canon.gate@almac.co.uk

All forms of payment are accepted and p&p is free to any address in the U.K. Please specify if you want to join the Rebel Inc. mailing list.

HUNGER

KNUT HAMSUN

A NEW TRANSLATION BY SVERRE LYNGSTAD
INTRODUCED BY DUNCAN MCLEAN

First published in 1890, Knut Hamsun's *Hunger* has come to be regarded as one of the major modernist novels, anticipating and influencing much fiction that was to follow. As with Joyce's *Ulysses*, the story itself is simple but the writing is multi-layered, challenging and linguistically stunning.

Set in the ostensible location of Kristiania (Oslo), *Hunger* is a compelling trip into the mind of a young writer, driven by starvation to constantly fluctuating extremes of euphoria and despair. It is a study of the psychological hinterlands - the very edges of experience - where few writers have the courage to tread.

"Never has the Nobel Prize been awarded to one worthier of it" **Thomas Mann**

"*Hunger* is an amazing book" **New Statesman**

"One of the most disturbing novels in existence" **Time Out**

"*Hunger* is undoubtedly one of the most important novels of the modern age. At last it has found a translator capable of doing justice to its immense power and complexity: Lyngstad's deserves to become the standard English version" **Duncan Mclean**

YOUNG ADAM

ALEXANDER TROCCHI
INTRODUCED BY JOHN PRINGLE

Alexander Trocchi's first novel is an existential thriller set on a barge travelling along the canal that runs between Glasgow and Edinburgh. What plot there is revolves around the discovery of the corpse of a young woman found floating in the canal.

As tensions develop between the narrator of the story - who discovers the body and whose relationship with the dead woman gradually unfolds - and the couple with whom he shares the cramped space on the barge, the reader is slowly sucked into the disturbed psyche of Trocchi's rootless anti-hero.

Drawing inspiration from Camus' *The Outsider*, *Young Adam*, like Trocchi himself, has been increasingly regarded as a lost 'gem' of Scottish literature. Out of print for years, this edition restores Trocchi's definitive version of the text and marks the first publication of a novel by Trocchi in his native land. It should also help to reassert Trocchi as one of Scotland's most neglected and talented post-war writers.

"*Young Adam* is a novel of unusally compelling quality"
The Herald

"A critical and pivotal figure in the literary world of the 1950s and 60s" **William Buroughs**

"A very fine writer" **Norman Mailer**

"Alexander Trocchi may be the greatest unknown writer in the world." **The Bloomsbury Review**

DRUGS AND THE PARTY LINE

KEVIN WILLIAMSON

WITH AN INTRODUCTION BY IRVINE WELSH

The use of recreational drugs has become the subject of an unprecedented national debate. Unfortunately the outbreak of media hysteria following the death of Leah Betts and others has provoked leading politicians into declaring a war on drugs.

Illegal drugs have been described as the new "enemy within" and drug-users equated with "a medieval plague". Any semblance of rational debate has been buried beneath the hysteria. The first casualty of any war is truth and for the war against drugs this has been no different.

Drugs and the Party Line aims to cut through the hysteria, hype and myths surrounding the use of recreational drugs in an accessible and informed way. Sticking to the facts, *Drugs and the Party Line* asks the questions that the politicians should really be addressing.

Unlike most books on the subject of drugs, *Drugs and the Party Line* not only answers these questions but puts forward a full political manifesto for changing existing drug laws based on progressive drug-specific policies of harm reduction, decriminalisation of drug-users, plus controlled availability for some drugs.